Tessa
The Boatyard Mystery

By

Adeline Setterfield

Copyright

ISBN 978-1-988719-15-3

Contents

1

Just for the Record

The accident happened five years ago. No one thought I would survive, but I did. My mom didn't make it, though. We were on our way to school when our car slid out of control on a patch of freakin' snow and that's all it took to end her life. I'll never forget waking up in hospital to see my dad sitting on a stool beside the bed. One hand covered his eyes while the other held my own, and I could feel the warmth of his fingers in mine. He must have sensed my stare because he looked up with a sudden jerk of the head and I saw his tear-streaked face—that's when I knew a life-changing event had taken place.

My life would never be the same again and neither would his. They say the brain is an amazing organ and it will compensate for functions lost due to injury, but I got more than I bargained for—not that anyone one else knows about it. Whether these gifts are a blessing or a curse is not for me to judge. Jinx, fifteen years old, thinks my acquired powers are just cray and a gift from God, but I doubt that—I don't believe in God. Well, not one who would take a young girl's mother from her, and that's just being bible. The truth is I do have some strange abilities few other people have, and definitely one that I'm sure no one else has: I can bend certain metals with my mind. I recently read about a man many years ago, who could bend spoons and forks by looking at them, but I kid you not, I can do better than that—I've actually slain construction grade rebar.

Another ability I seemed to have acquired was to see things about people. I could do this if I had an item of clothing, or a wristwatch, some personal material of theirs to touch. These cray phenomena started the week following the accident and had grown in their effectiveness over the years. Jinx knew because he found out one day by accident—we won't go into that because it was embarrassing for me. I would never tell my dad about it because he would freak out and have me examined by all sorts of people who really don't know their asses from their elbows. Luke Tamburrino was my dad, and the current sheriff of Falcon Ridge. He unknowingly benefitted from my abilities from time to time because when I put my mind to it, I solved crimes the police couldn't. I always did it in a way that placed the most damning evidence in dad's hands and I was sure even he thought it was either a lucky break or he was one very sick fellow.

At eighteen years old, I had been accused of being a bit tomboyish. I probably was not typical of my so-called millennial generation who spent a good deal of their time on phones because I loved the outdoors. I used the technology like everyone else my age, but I had also discovered there were other things in life. My body was undergoing change, filling out in the usual places, but I hadn't felt all that much attracted to boys yet. I believed by this age I was supposed to be mad about them, but I think dad would have a fit if I brought one home. My dad thought I was pretty. He loved my dark hair to be short and frankly I preferred it like that myself. My mom used to say I inherited her genes, her blue eyes, her shape, her temperament, and maybe she was right—except for one thing: I saw myself as calm and introvert, more like my dad. Mom loved the social life and I often felt she could have become a debutante or something like that.

Most girls my age fought a lot amongst themselves and said ugly things about each other on social media, but apart from Bree and Jan, I tended to stick to myself a lot. Perhaps it was because, since the accident I never went back to a conventional school. I was privately tutored.

I'm not obsessed with my weight. I watched what I ate, of course, but didn't go overboard on all the "good food" crap. Shopping was another thing girls go crazy about. They obsessed about the latest fashions and although a certain amount of fashion consciousness crossed my mind I still loved my old comfortable, outdoor clothes.

Besides my cat, Sheba, my dog, Twaddle and childhood classmates, Bree and Jan, Jinx Henderson was my only other friend. People would say Jinx was from the wrong side of the tracks and spoke badly—they wouldn't be far wrong. He was just a product of his environment and deeply influenced by the way his buddies spoke at school. Jinx and I were pretty tight, but don't worry, there was nothing going on between us.

I missed my mom. Dad was great, but there were things about me only another woman would understand. There were times I wanted to tell him about my unusual abilities, but then I realized it would change the nature of our relationship. My discovery of the effectiveness of my talents came about a year after the accident when I read a newspaper report about a local robbery. The owner of a small factory had been found unconscious in his office; the safe had been opened and all the money was missing. Scant details made it difficult for the police to find the robber and the owner never saw his assailant.

To cut a long story short, my psychic ability led to the arrest of a factory worker through clues my dad received from an anonymous source—me. My assessments were hundo P. Since then I have solved a few smaller cases in the same way, but one day dad arrived home, threw a file onto the dining room table and went to shower. I picked the file up and had a quick look. The photo of a woman peered up at me, a lady I knew well—Mrs. Evelyn Larson. I made a quick photocopy of the detail sheet.

Ж

2

My friend Jinx

My dad and I always had breakfast together as a matter of principle rather than ritual. I did most of the cooking because he was not very domesticated. He did, however, do his best. I knew he went to boarding school for a good deal of his young academic life, and he told me the food was very structured—I might have survived the cooks at a boarding school, but his culinary attempts were more often a disaster than not—just saying. Don't get me wrong—I loved my dad, but he should stay out of the kitchen. I was more than happy to cook the meals.

I passed him the salt. "You staying home this afternoon?" he asked.

I nodded my head and shoveled egg into my mouth.

After the accident, dad took me out of school and paid for a private home tutor. I had missed six months due to various operations on my head and normal schooling didn't work at the time anyway, for obvious reasons. My tutor, Miss Bennett, and I were reasonably tight, but sometimes she tried to play mother and my struggle became real. One thing was totally perf though—I had the afternoons to myself.

Dad sipped on his coffee. "You're going out? Where?"

Endless questions.

"I'm meeting Jinx down at the old quarry."

"You know I don't like you going there."

"I'll be safe—I'm taking Twaddle."

Nobody in their right mind would try anything stupid while my dog is around. They wouldn't get within two steps of me. Only Jinx, of course. Twaddle, Jinx and I were like a squad. Most people didn't trust pit bulls, but Twaddle was my shadow and where I went, he went—or tried to go. I'd had him for three years, since a pup. He was obedient and strong with the heart of a lion.

"Okay, but try to be home by four. How's Miss Bennett?"

"She's good. I still think you and her would make a good match."

"I already told you, sweetheart—she's a bit young for me. Besides, I have you and my job. Both take up all the free time I have."

"Age is just a number, dad. I can tell she likes you whenever you grace us with your presence. You should ask her out one day."

My dad shot me a look that would have frightened even Twaddle. "I don't need a matchmaker, Tessa. I'm quite happy as I am."

One letter added to my name was a definite expression of his annoyance.

"Talk about moving on with one's life," I mumbled.

'What did you say, honey?"

"Forget it, dad—just thinking out aloud. It's been over five years since mom died."

"Consider the conversation closed. I must get to work." He picked up the case file, walked around to my side of the table and kissed me on the head. "I'll see you later this afternoon."

I waited for him to leave before going into my room to pull out the photocopies I'd made of the file's details. Dad would murder me if he knew, but I deemed it one of those secrets from which he inevitably benefitted—not just him, but the entire law-enforcement community. The doorbell rang. Miss Bennett was on time.

*

I picked Jinx up at 2:30 p.m. as arranged and we drove down to the old quarry. There is a ledge on the North end, which allows us to approach small lake inside for a fall of about thirty feet to the water and all the kids use it in the summer. The air was cooler and the first leaves of the approaching fall already lay on the ground. Twaddle lay nearby, his watchful eyes fixed on me. Every time I looked at him, he thumped his tail on the ground a few times to let me know everything was under control.

Jinx lay on his back with his phone in hand, scrutinizing some messages from one of his pals. At fifteen, he passed for a kid at least two years his senior. His lanky frame and bony shoulders still waited a good amount of flesh which I assured him would come in his later years.

Our friendship began about a year after the accident. I found myself confronted by two boys on the way home from Bree's place one afternoon. These two particular wankstas were after more than basic things. Their roughneck manner and foul-mouthed oaths gave their intentions away—just another bunch of noobs. They passed lurid comments with obscene gestures and made it evident they were up to no good. I wanted to turn and run in the opposite direction but knew they would easily catch me.

My greatest impediment, other than my false sense of pride, is another legacy from the accident—a prosthetic leg. I didn't run very fast—it was one of the reasons I said a positive thing about myself when I woke up every morning and looked in the mirror, a kind of compliment if you like. The leg was also a reason I could never wear a dress.

The one boy stood directly in my path while the other walked past and turned in behind me. I stopped, frightened and angry at the same time.

"Pull up your top and show me those fleshy, little boobs," he said.

"Go and wank behind a tree," I returned.

He slapped me hard through the face and I burst into tears. The other boy grabbed me from behind and tried to slip his hands beneath my top. I wriggled out of his grasp and that's when I got my first sight of Jinx—a tall child for his age, thin and lanky, but determined. While sitting on the verandah of his home, it became evident what the two wankstas were up to. He grabbed a baseball bat, rushed out into the road and came up from behind. Jinx swung the bat with all his strength and caught the boy behind me, a heavy blow on the back of the head. The dickhead in front of me got such a fright he could only stand and gawk at his fallen friend while Jinx, almost frothing at the mouth, pushed me out of the way and stepped up to whack him a shot.

An adult in an adjacent yard on the street came out of her house and saw what was happening. She shouted at the two idiots and the one in front of me turned to make a run for it, but not before Jinx caught him with a glancing blow with the bat. The first boy managed to get back onto his feet, still groggy from the blow, staggering around like he was turnt. My knight in shining armor rounded on him for the second time and the dick's bravado deserted him. The two idiots both fled the scene and left me standing there in tears.

"Are you, like, okay? I didn't like, mean to scare you." It was a sorry not sorry thing.

"You didn't frighten me—you saved me," I said.

From that day on, we've been tight. He is not the best looking boy I have ever seen, but what he lacks in looks he makes up for in personality. Although everyone called him Jinx his real name was Jerry. The name, Jinx, apparently stuck after his dad had told friends that the family's lives had become jinxed after the boy's birth.

The quarry's quiet atmosphere dissolved with a loud bird call, which sounded out across the lake, and Jinx tore his eyes away from his phone for a second. "You say you know this missing woman?"

"She's the wife of Kurt Larson, the guy who owns the boatyard."

"Did they, like...have an argument or something?"

I gazed out across the quarry. "Not according to Mr. Larson. He has no idea what happened to her."

Jinx tapped away for a few more seconds, sent off the text he'd been working on and then looked up at me.

"Maybe she got, like, tired of him."

"Maybe, but then she would just leave him and go to her mother's, or something like that. She wouldn't disappear altogether."

"True—but perhaps she had a creeper."

"I don't know, but my dad is on the case. As far as I can see, the police have asked around and followed up on a few leads, but so far they've been owned."

"I know what you're thinking, dude."

"What?"

"We should, like, look into it." He slipped his phone into his pocket.

I laughed. "You know, Jinx—for a fifteen-year-old, you're sick."

"Yolo," he said.

Ж

3

The Larson Property

Half an hour later, we decided to leave the quarry and check out the Larson's address. I knew Mrs. Larson from the local Girl-Guide's association when I used to be a member prior to the accident. She looked after a group of girls and taught wilderness survival techniques. I remembered her as a very cool type of person, a driving force in the annual cookie drive campaigns and felt sad at the thought some harm might have befallen her. I determined in my heart to make a contribution to the case in whatever way possible.

My old Jeep bumped and groaned in agony along the quarry road. We almost lost Twaddle a few times but he managed somehow to keep his balance and stay in the vehicle. Jinx always complained that I drove like his granny, but as a new driver, I always did my best to obey the rules of the road. I knew the first thing I wanted to do if the opportunity availed itself was to find something personal to Mrs. Larson; anything she deemed important or an item of her clothing. Not everything works. In fact, I'm not sure what works, and often

I have tried things that normally should have worked, but didn't. They had a childless marriage and both worked all day, with Mrs. Larson in the boatyard office and Mr. Larson out fishing. If Jinx and I could get into the garage or the house to find something I could use, it would be helpful.

"Do you think it's safe to like poke around on the Larson property?" shouted Jinx. The wind noise from the Jeep's open cockpit made it difficult to be heard.

"I'm sure it'll be fine. She's missing and he spends all his day at the boat business. There may be something in an outhouse or the garage."

Twaddle squeezed in between us, looked at me first and then at Jinx. I turned to glance at his yellow, lion eyes and he, in turn, gave two short barks of approval. When Jinx turned his head he received a load of saliva across the left ear. Twaddle's brindle coat glistened in the bright sunlight and the white blaze, which started under his muzzle as a narrow streak and ended in a wide patch on his broad chest, looking like a flag of truce.

I found the address and parked at the curb. The house, a colonial styled affair with red brick face and slate roof, gave the impression of considerable wealth. We got out and walked down the drive to the backyard area where the car garage nestled among several large oak trees. I saw some cardboard boxes against the inner wall of an attached carport. Twaddle, excited to be in a new place raced around sniffing at the base of all the trees, ecstatic to read the fido news of whatever resident dogs existed in the area.

"Let's see if there's anything in those boxes," I said.

We opened the first box to discover some old crockery, no longer in fashion and supposedly placed into storage. The second box contained what I had hoped to find—old souvenirs and an old photo of a young woman in a silver-lined frame. The glass overlay was broken.

"This may be useful," I said.

Jinx stared over my shoulder. "She's pretty—do you like, think it's her?"

"It's her all right." I removed the photo and placed the frame back into the box. The reaction came with an immediate sensation of dread. I bowed my head and allowed the photo to take me wherever it needed to. The sound of rushing wind filled my ears and a mist seemed to billow out of the photo to engulf me. Jinx disappeared from view and with the sudden effect, I could see a scene of which I became a part.

The room was familiar and I knew I had been in it before—the boatyard reception office. In front of me stood a man with a long scar down his left cheek and a brown wool toque on his head. He also wore a thin, brown sweater with a polar neck and the look in his dark black eyes struck fear into my heart. He reached out to grab me and his fingers closed around my neck with the strength of a vice. The savage shouted something at me, but no sound came from his lips—just those dark black eyes, like two burning coals in a blacksmith's forge, piercing right through me. I cringed and tried to struggle out of the grip but his hands tightened and I began to feel faint. I tried to cry out, but no sound came. He dragged my body out of the office and onto the boardwalk, which I knew led to the adjacent wharf. I tried to cry out again but my words were lost in the rushing sound of the wind. One of the fishing vessels appeared and he continued to drag me on board. That's when I passed out.

I woke up at the sound of a voice. "Cripes, Tess —don't do that, again. You like, scared the crap out of me, dude," said Jinx.

I smiled weakly, still feeling the effects of my psychic transportation. "It'll do you some good," I said. "You're so full of it anyway."

He grinned and yanked me up into a sitting position. It would appear I collapsed under the intensity and power of the vision. This never happened before and I felt scared. I told Jinx what I had seen.

He looked dumbfounded. "Are you sure you didn't just like, imagine this?"

"I know what I saw, dude," I said. Anger at his doubtful attitude overshadowed the moment. I hate it when someone won't believe what I tell them. "I would never lie to you. You know this happens to me."

He looked a bit sheepish and pulled out his phone for comfort. "Sorry, Tess. It just came like, as a surprise is all. I know you see things but you've never like, passed out before. I was scared for you."

Twaddle started a licking frenzy again, so I grabbed him around the neck and held him tightly to me. I guess he, too, felt a measure of uncertainty at my actions.

"Let's get out of here," I said.

We walked back to the Jeep in silence. Twaddle wouldn't leave my side and kept getting tangled up with my prosthetic leg until I picked up a branch and threw it for him to fetch. He needed the distraction.

I dropped Jinx off at his home. "See you tomorrow afternoon?" he asked.

I answered with a vague tone. "Sure, dude."

"You okay, Tess?"

"Yep," I answered. "Bye, Felicia."

He nodded and I pulled away, lost in my own thoughts.

Once back at home, I went through the mental notes I had made of the Larson case. None of the leads meant much in real terms. I would need to research Kurt Larson's staff, so I did what I always do when I need information, went onto the Internet and Googled, "Larson and Petrov Boatyard."

The website came up under "Larson and Petrov Boat Repairs and Industrial Fishing, Ltd."

A full description of the business revealed nothing of importance but I did get to see Sam Petrov's face. Petrov was Kurt Larson's business partner—it wasn't him—the man with the scar I saw in my vision. I kept reading, but nothing of consequence leaped out of the details. They had been in partnership for eight years and seemed to be busy enough to be making money. Again, I reflected on what I saw while holding the old photograph of Mrs. Larson in my hand earlier that afternoon.

I saw the face of her abductor but could prove nothing with regard to his involvement in the crime; no one would believe me if I told them. Frustrated, I decided to dipnet and check my Facebook. Several of the girls with whom I am Facebook friends were having a squabble about a boy who had dated them, but I refrained from making any posts and decide to have a quick shower before dad arrived home. I went to the bathroom, removed my leg and got undressed. The hot water felt good on my skin, and a good soak did wonders to dismiss the afternoon's tension. A sudden thought came to me—kind of weird, almost as if a voice whispered a sentence in my ear. Had I imagined it or was my mind playing tricks on me?

Again the voice whispered, *"There's more."*

I felt a little light-headed and foolish. The few times this gift operated since its inception after the accident had been more like an incidental dream and I had never experienced anything like this before.

The voice came again. *"There's more."*

"What do you mean?" I uttered. My voice shook with emotion and now, apparently I was talking to myself.

I shouted out aloud. "More what?"

Silence.

Suddenly it became obvious what needed to be done. I toweled myself off, dressed and attached my leg. The old photo lay on my dresser top and hesitation had my hand hovering over it, uncertain if it should be touched. But it had to be done. With a flinch, I remembered the dinner and turned away. Preparation of the food would take only ten minutes and while it cooked, I would return to take up the photo and find out what more lay in store.

The frozen pork steaks needed to be defrosted first and while they heated in the microwave, preparation of the vegetables for steaming took up the remainder of the time.

Ten minutes later, I returned to the room and stared at the photo. In the silence that followed, the voice spoke again. *"There's more,"* it whispered.

I looked around my bedroom in shock. It sounded like a woman's voice, but no one materialized.

I picked up the photo and held it to my breast. Then the air around me became electrified and a coldness seeped into my bones.

Ж

4

The Man with the Scarred Cheek

A flash of light seared across my mind's eye, followed by a jarring and a bumping, as if my body was being dragged across a wooden floor or deck. Then I remembered. This is where my experience had terminated in the afternoon before my loss of consciousness. The man with the scarred cheek dragged my body onto one of the fishing boats, lifted it up over the rim of a hatch and a sudden free-fall ended with a jarring thud. The cold surface contained hundreds of small cubes—ice.

My muscles wouldn't obey me and the atmosphere became quite chilly. In the limited light, no condensation from my breath rose into the air above. *Odd,*I thought. Then it became evident— there would be no condensation of breath because Mrs. Larson was dead.

*

I awoke out of the stupor to find myself lying on the floor of the bedroom and for a moment confusion reigned. Then it came to me. Mrs. Larson was no longer alive. I felt an enormous depression flow over my soul like thick oil. I wept for many minutes until the oven's alarm chimed the end of its preheat stage for the pork. It took great effort to raise myself off the floor and limp to the kitchen to finish off the dinner preparations.

The front door opened and dad walked in throwing the late afternoon newspaper onto the dining room table.

"Hi, Tess. How's your day been?"

"Okay, I guess," I murmured.

He looked at my face and saw something had upset me. "What's wrong, honey. You look so sad."

I hadn't had enough time to regain my composure and it showed.

"I'm sad about Mrs. Larson."

He looked at me in surprise. "How do you know about Mrs. Larson? It's only just come out on the news this evening."

I thought quickly. "Jinx heard it from someone."

Dad shook his head. "I'm amazed how bad news gets around so quickly."

"She used to teach me when I did guides," I said.

"Yeah. It's a bad scene. She's just disappeared into thin air."

I wanted to tell him but the words stuck in my throat. I wanted him to know that a man with a scarred cheek killed her and dumped her on ice in a fishing vessel, but I caught myself just in time. He would more than likely have me certified.

"I'm not feeling so well, dad. I'm going to my room—the food's ready."

I ran out of the kitchen without dishing up and his stare followed after me.

"Tess, honey—are you okay?"

I reached my bedroom as the tears started to course down my cheeks.

"Yeah. I'll be all right. I just need a little time on my own."

I closed the bedroom door, threw myself onto the bed and did my best to stifle the sobs. I wanted my mom so bad. The whole experience had been too much for me. I had learned that my gifts came with a hardship and a responsibility but acceptance never comes easily. They have a downside and an upside, neither of which I wanted, but the choice to discard them wasn't mine to make.

An hour later my dad knocked on the door. "Can I come in?" he asked.

By this time, my composure had returned. "It's not locked."

He tentatively opened the door and peered into the room. "Just wanted to see if you're all right."

Twaddle brushed past dad's legs, jumping up onto the bed and making himself comfortable. His lion eyes held mine for a few seconds, followed by two short coughs.

"I'm fine. It came as a shock. I'll be okay," I said. "Do you have people out searching for her?"

"We have every cop in Falcon Ridge looking for her, honey. I'm sure someone will come up with something."

I wanted to tell him to look inside one of the fishing trawlers—that a horrible man with a scar had murdered her, but again the words would not form in my mouth.

"Thanks for dinner," he said.

"You're welcome. Sorry, you had to dish it up yourself."

"Not a problem, get a good night's sleep." He closed the door and left me in peace.

*

In the morning I woke to the feel of a paw on my cheek. Sheba, my cat, squinted into my eyes and meowed her usual, "good morning, get up; the sun has already risen, why the hell are you still in bed," greeting.

"Shove off, Sheba. Leave me alone," I mumbled. The paw became persistent. My defense lay in the turn-over routine but Sheba would not be put off. A moment later the paw pushed on my cheek again. Twaddle lifted his head, eyed the cat with intent and then thumped his tail a few times on the bed to let me know he had my back.

I pushed Sheba away and sat up. The previous day's memories came flooding back and with it a measure of depression. A way had to be found to bring my dad's attention to the real facts. But how could this be done? Some investigation would be required after my morning's schooling session with Miss Bennett—Jinx had indicated he would be available. I needed to check out the staff members plus the two fishing trawlers, which belonged to the Larson and Petrov boat business. My scant knowledge of boats needed to be supplemented, but one thing I did know: the hatch to the storage area which kept the catch cold—the place where Scar Cheek dumped the body—existed somewhere on the deck behind the main cabin.

I slipped on my leg, got dressed and recited my ritual before the mirror. It was something I read online: "When you accept your flaws no one can use them against you." It helped me to get the day going right on a good footing, to hear the words come out of my mouth. Twaddle thought it time for a game and grabbed one of my rides. This ended in a tug of war between the two of us until I shouted at him to let go. He gave me the hurt look and then grinned, which was achieved by a pulled-up lip and bared front teeth—it's really quite cute—and all was forgiven. The wall calendar revealed it to be Tuesday, porridge day, but an empty container meant dad and I would be having cereal. Time to go to the grocery store again.

Dad came in and sat down at the table while I checked the messages on my phone. "Feeling any better this morning, cupcake?"

"Yep, I'm over it," I lied. The vision still plagued me like a bad dream.

"I'm sure we'll find her," he said.

We ate breakfast and he left for work. Miss Bennett arrived on cue and the morning dragged on with Roman history. To my relief 12:30 p.m. arrived at which time Miss Bennett left. It was not that I found the schoolwork boring, but my need to investigate Mrs. Larson's murder took center stage, and my efforts needed to get underway.

I picked Jinx up at his home and drove toward the wharf. The old Jeep kept misfiring and emitting puffs of smoke from the exhaust, which caused bystanders some concern as to its roadworthiness, but we just laughed at the looks on their faces.

With the Jeep parked beyond the boatyard entrance and Twaddle given the command to "stay", we walked onto the premises for a look around. The yard, open to the general public, exemplified a typical boat repair business with lots of small skiffs and rowboats on blocks in some form of repair. The main office seemed the best place to start. Neither of us knew exactly what we were looking for, but I hoped for some sort of noticeboard upon which staff members might be depicted, or that we might see some of them in the office. I saw only one of the trawlers at the wharf. It was our hope the staff would be going about their general duties.

Mr. Larson stood behind the counter in the main office. I guess he had taken over his wife's job until they could find out what happened to her —of course, I knew she wouldn't be coming back, but maybe Mr. Larson didn't.

There were two other people in the office, one whom I took to be a customer and the other appeared to be a staff member, at a guess, an old man in his late sixties. Pictures of boats and ships lined one of the walls. Jinx and I inspected each one while we kept a lookout for staff members. A man walked in from the back of the building and went to talk to Mr. Larson. I nearly wet myself. The man with the scarred cheek—the same toque and brown sweater. He wore dirty blue jeans, held up with an old leather belt and filthy dark brown, leather boots—it was him.

I grabbed Jinx's arm and pulled him in front of me in an effort to hide from the murderer's eyes.

"It's him," I whispered, my voice sounding a bit raspy. Jinx shot me a questioning glance and then looked in the direction of the counter.

"That man with Mr. Larson—it's him—the murderer."

I heard Jinx's sharp intake of breath as he spotted Scar Cheek. The man spoke to Mr. Larson and then turned to leave. He glanced in our direction and I felt the coal black eyes rake me like a scythe. Mr. Larson must have remembered something because he called to out to Scar Cheek, who had walked off down the passageway to the rear of the building.

"Oh, Benny—one more thing..."

Scar Cheek aka Benny did a quick turn-about and hurried back to the counter. They talked for another minute and then Scar Cheek left again, but this time through the front door of the office. My stomach started to heave. It's as though he had violated me with his stare. The vision returned with its violence and I saw myself looking up at the inside of the hatch door and not seeing the condensate of my own breath in the cold air, all over again.

"Let's get out of here. I've seen enough," I said.

Jinx grabbed my arm. "We should...um, like, check the trawlers before we...um, go, dude."

My whole body trembled at the thought of remaining on the premises for one more second, but he was right. We came to investigate and although I now knew Scar Cheek, or Benny as he had been called worked for the boat company, I still needed to know if Mrs. Larson's body lay in the fishing trawler's hold. We left through the front entrance of the office and walked around the corner of the building to the wharf. I saw no sign of Benny and my confidence returned. No one else appeared to be on the trawler, so we jumped off the wharf and onto the boat's deck. In the middle of the vessel, I could see a raised section with a hatch.

I crept toward the hatch with my heart in my mouth. Jinx struck out toward the main cabin, which led into the wheelhouse. He opened the door and peered inside. I steeled myself to open the hatch and tried to keep my lunch down. What would happen if Mrs. Larson's body lay at the bottom of the hold? I reached down, grabbed the handle and pulled with all my strength. The hatch door opened easily and I stared down into the void. Enough light poured in through the opening for me to see all the way to the bottom—empty.

Instant relief overtook me and I staggered back to the boat's gunnel. At the same time, Jinx returned from the wheelhouse and we looked at each other.

"Was she like, in there, dude?" he asked.

I shook my head. "See anything in the wheel-house?"

"Nope. Just the steering wheel and radio. Nothing like, out of the ordinary."

"There's still another trawler," I said.

Jinx shrugged. "We'll have to like, come back when it's here."

On our return to the Jeep, Twaddle jumped up onto the driver's seat and gave his two customary cough-like barks. I shooed him into the back and we drove off in the direction of home.

"What're you going to like, do, dude?" asked Jinx. He pulled out his phone and checked the latest message.

"I've been thinking. They wouldn't leave her in the hold for long. It would be too dangerous. As much as I hated to do it, I needed to consult with her photo again."

Ж

5

Sam Petrov

After dinner prep, I gave Twaddle his bowl of biscuits and sat down with Sheba on my lap to watch some telly. Our local news featured Mrs. Larson's disappearance and showed a tearful Kurt Larson make an appeal to the public for any relevant information. A twinge of guilt-riddled my conscience but the probability of me being laughed out of Falcon Ridge dealt with the urge to share my experience. The best and only way would be to get firm proof and then feed it to my dad.

Perhaps one day he would catch on to the real source of the clues, but until that happened, it seemed better to let sleeping dogs lie. A further consultation with Mrs. Larson's photo still might give more insight as to the whereabouts of her body. After watching the news, I returned to my bedroom. The photo lay in the drawer of my dresser and the moment my fingers touched it, the voice whispered again. *"There's more."*

For a moment my courage deserted me, but with final resolution and accompanied by a heavy sigh of resignation, my nerves became obedient to the quest. I took up the photo and held it to my breast. The surroundings merged with a sudden mistiness and it felt as though my being flowed like a liquid through a pipe. It accelerated at a fast pace until it slowed down with a sudden lurch and I could see the open hatch of the trawler's hold above me. A long pole with a hook on the one end —I think it's called a gaff—snagged my body and lifted it up through the opening and onto the deck where I lay for a few seconds. At the sound of a splash, I sensed water all around me. Bubbles of air escaped rapidly past my vision. The surroundings darkened and without warning my senses plunged into blackness, followed by the rush of return to full consciousness, and I surfaced from the mistiness to my bedroom's surrounding again.

The photo still clutched firmly in my hands felt warm as I stood there for another minute in contemplation of what had been revealed. The realization hit me hard—Mrs. Larson had been dumped overboard, somewhere in deep water and no one would ever find her body. A dark, brooding cloud of depression swept over me again. I threw myself onto the bed, determined not to cry, but tears won in the end. The thought of Mrs. Larson's violent end created a huge knot in my stomach, and for a moment I thought I might throw up all over the duvet.

After a determined effort to gain control, I sat up to wipe the tears away from my eyes. My dad should not be allowed to see me in such a state for the second time. Sheba brushed up against my leg as cats often do and I grabbed her for a comfort cuddle. She purred contentedly until Twaddle jumped onto the bed with us and stuck his snout into my face. Sanity returned and I felt a bit better.

I heard dad enter through the front door and open the entrance closet to deposit his jacket. "Tess, I'm home."

By the time he arrived in the kitchen, the dinner had found its way onto the dining room table and he received his customary peck on the cheek. "How's your day been, dad?"

"Not bad, honey. Still tied up with the Larson case."

"Any leads?" I asked. We sat down at the table and I picked up my phone to check my texts.

"Nothing of any consequence. We have established, though, she left the boathouse in a hurry. Mr. Larson discovered she failed to close off the till and do things that should have been done by the end of the day's business. Nobody saw her leave the premises. We have questioned all the staff and nobody knows anything."

Again, the urge to blurt out my experience caught in my throat, but I laced up and smiled. "I'm sure something will come to light," I said.

While we ate, I thought I would test the waters. "Have you ever thought of consulting a psychic, dad?"

He looked up from his plate of food and grimaced. "Psychics are just charlatans, honey. I won't be consulting anyone like that for official police business, I can assure you." He must have seen the look of disdain on my face. "Oh come on, Tessa. You can't be serious?"

"I'm just saying."

"I'd be laughed out of the department," he said.

"I know the feeling," I returned.

"Well, maybe it's something Mr. Larson might do, but me—never."

The struggle was real. I thought of the many clues he had received via my psychic ability and almost choked on my food. My face went red as it usually does when I'm angry and felt owned.

"I've heard of psychics helping other police departments out. What's so damn different about Falcon Ridge?"

He fixed me with an obstinate stare. "Take it easy, Tessa. There's no need to get annoyed. I'm simply saying I would not use such people to help find a missing person. My guess is they just got lucky."

I realized my dad was just being a noob. It wouldn't help to antagonize him—the best thing for me and for the case was to keep my mouth shut. One day, at the right time he would know the truth and as they say, the truth will set him free. I carried on eating in silence and when we were finished with dinner, he wiped his mouth with a napkin. "You always do such a wonderful job with the dinner. Your mother taught you well."

I wanted to tell him not to patronize me but instead, again, I laced up.

"Thanks, dad. You're welcome."

"I don't know what I'd do without you, honey. It scares the hell out of me that one day you'll meet someone and start your own family. It's only natural."

"I'm only eighteen, dad. That day is still far away—if it ever comes."

My dad came around to my side of the table and hugged me. "I know we don't see eye to eye on things sometimes, cupcake, but you know I love you more than anything in the whole world, right?"

I felt bad about my previous thoughts. "I know you do, dad. You must also miss mom terribly—I do."

I could see the tears form in his eyes. "More than anyone will ever know, darling."

I volunteered to wash up and he left the dining room to pour himself a whiskey. By 8:30 p.m., I heard him snoring away in his chair in front of the telly.

Telling him about my abilities would be completely out of the question. Perf. I could do it on my own. After a shower, I retired to my room to check my Facebook and messages.

A text from Bree: *So fed up with my mom's constant meddling. Sometimes I feel like canceling her.*

I texted her back: *Be glad you've got a mom. I would welcome it.*

The answer came back a few moments later:

Sorry, Tess. I know you miss your mom, but my mine is interfering in everything.

I kind of understood her plight. My dad trusted me with all my online stuff but he did ask a lot of questions about what Jinx and I did when we were together.

Give her a break, dude. She's just worried about you, I answered.

I know. It's just at times she's so cray and suspicious of everything I do.

Don't worry, be happy. Going to bed now. Talk to u lader.

The answer came back: *Bye, Felicia.*

Twaddle and Sheba piled onto the bed as I turned the light out. A question came to mind: what must I do next? How would I find proof, other than my psychic knowledge, to point the finger in Scar Cheek's direction? At some point, the investigation would bog down without the presence of a body and the case might be considered as cold. I had to figure something out.

My phone pinged—a text from Jan:

Just watched the latest Timberlake concert online.

How fickle, I thought.

*

Miss Bennett arrived the following morning with a rap on the door, which sent Twaddle into his usual barking frenzy. It was a game to him and although he knew exactly who stood at the door, he treated the whole event like the coming apocalypse. His tail would wag at hurricane rate and no matter how loud I shouted at him, he would rush out the moment the door opened and make his mock attack. Fortunately, Miss Bennett, an animal lover, took it all in her stride and tolerated his antics with good humor.

The morning passed quickly with tests in English comprehension, mathematics, and Physics, all subjects I enjoyed. Miss Bennett laid out homework for the next day and come 12:30 p.m., she left. Jinx had things to do at home, so I decided to take Twaddle out for a walk and give the Larson case some more thought. I needed to find something else that would lead me further into the life of Evelyn Larson. I took off in the direction of their residence a distance of several miles with no specific plan in mind. Due to a lack of talcum powder, my stump rubbed a little in the prosthetic's harness, and I made a mental note to stop at the corner store on the way back for more.

Twaddle loved going for walks and made a thorough nuisance of himself as he rushed here, there and everywhere. I didn't want to restrict him with a leash because he's reasonably obedient and will listen when I call—well, most times. I thought about the boxes Jinx and I found in the Larson's carport. If I could find an item more recent than the photo, it may tell me something more.

One hour later, Twaddle and I approached the Larson's home. It looked deserted and after a quick check for nosey neighbors, I decided to take the plunge. The boxes were still where Jinx and I left them, however, another two large boxes had been added to the stack. These containers were in better shape than the others and I hoped they contained more recent items. Anything relevant to the case would be welcome.

Twaddle struck off to investigate the various tree-trunk bases for messages and left me to continue my search. I gave no thought for any danger and became engrossed in searching through the first box when I heard a noise behind me. On turning my head to investigate, a pair of strong hands gripped my shoulders from behind and swiveled me around. I nearly fainted. Sam Petrov, Mr. Larson's business partner stood there and glared into my eyes.

"What are you doing? Looking for stuff to steal?" He sounded angry and gripped my arms so tightly I felt them go numb.

"I'm...ah...sorry. I was just curious," I stammered.

"What's your name?" His eyes bore into me like lasers and I could feel myself going into shock.

A strange thing happened right at that moment. The sudden rush of the wind and a billowy mist that I often experience when I see things, appeared to engulf the two of us. I could feel myself being transported to another place and then the motion stopped in a room. I recognized two people sitting on a love seat, about to smooch each other. Their closed eyes and expectant lips projected the timeless story of two lovers who meet under clan-

destine circumstances to further an illicit relationship. I realized this to be the case—the couple was
Mr. Petrov and Mrs. Larson.

As their lips met, the scene dissolved in a flash
of light and I felt my mind return to the unwel-
come circumstances.

Mr. Petrov still held me by the arms and his
eyes continued to hold mine, as though locked in
mortal combat. He shook me again.

"Tell me who you are and what you're doing
here?" he shouted.

I didn't want to let him know who I was. That
would open up a huge can of worms for me. I
struggled to get free. "Let me go, you stupid noob,"
I screamed.

My good foot lashed out and caught him below
the left knee. It angered him and he lifted his hand
to hit me, but never quite launched the blow.
Twaddle, bless his lion heart, returned from
amongst the bushes at the back of the yard and at-
tacked Petrov from behind.

He screamed as Twaddle took hold of his ankle
and pulled the leg sideways. Petrov's pants ripped
and Twaddle let go with the hope of a better hold
on the leg. He succeeded in sinking his teeth into
the man's calf. My attacker let go of me and looked
around wildly for something with which he could
defend himself. Twaddle's yellow-green eyes fol-

lowed his quarry's movements and then rushed in again to catch Petrov by the other leg. The poor man couldn't find anything to protect himself with and fell down onto his knees. I knew I had to intervene. A pit bull is most dangerous when protecting his own and I was his pack.

I reached in, grabbed the dog's collar and pulled with all my might. Twaddle, almost turned on me in his surprise but realized who it was at the last moment. I shouted at him to follow and ran as fast as the prosthesis would allow. My jeans hid the fact of a false leg, so I did my best to run as smoothly as possible in hopes Petrov would not notice my impediment. Twaddle made one final mock lunge at him and then turned to follow after me. We sprinted out of the yard and down the street toward the park on the corner. A shortcut through the trees and bushes would take us in the direction of the shop I had intended to visit on the way back home.

Once in the park and amongst the trees, I stopped to catch my breath. Twaddle raced around in circles as though it was all a game. I sat at the base of a tree to catch my breath and received a deluge of licks.

"Good boy, Twaddle. Good boy." His tail oscillated like a windshield wiper.

Without his intervention, I don't know what would have happened.

I pulled out my phone and sent a quick text to Jinx. *Just had a huge scare.*

The answer came back in seconds: *Whaddap, dude?*

I couldn't contain my excitement. *Just had a meeting with Sam Petrov. Caught me sniffing around Larson's place.*

Who's Sam P?

Larson's partner. Twaddle saved me.

Find anything?

I'll tell ya lader, I answered.

After five minutes of rest, I recovered and we took the path through to the other side of the park.

Reflection on the latest revelation provided much food for thought.

Ж

6

The Stakeout

After dinner, I sat in the living room with my phone in hand and made small talk with dad while he read the evening newspaper.

"You're pretty subdued tonight, dad."

He lowered the paper to look at me. "I'm just a little frustrated at the lack of progress on the Larson case. We have nothing—a woman disappears into thin air and there is not even a trace."

"Have you considered she may have boarded one of the trawlers," I asked.

"It's possible, but we've questioned the crew of the boats and although everyone is a suspect, they deny any wrongdoing. Both boats came up clean under an inspection."

"Maybe you should be asking for help," I said.

"Please don't bring up that psychic nonsense again, Tessa. You know how I feel about that. We've searched their home for clues, even Mr. Larson's partner, Mr. Petrov's home came under scrutiny, but there is simply nothing. I hate to say this but if something has happened to her, it would be better for us to find the body. We can do a lot with a body—DNA and so on."

"What about Mrs. Larson's private life? Might she have been involved in an affair or something like that? Maybe her husband found out."

My dad lowered the newspaper, glanced over the page and gave me a wry smile. "We've thought of all the angles, Tess. Let's not talk any more about it."

I nodded and brooded on in silent reflection of the afternoon's discovery. Two pieces of the puzzle, which could blow the case wide open, existed in a form that delivered no proof. My psychic ability carried only my word and I knew neither would be enough for the police to work with. Benny would deny any wrongdoing and Mr. Petrov would certainly not implicate himself in admission to an affair with Mrs. Larson. Logic told me Mr. Larson could be suspect if he found out his wife had cheated on him. I needed to establish a link between Mrs. Larson and Mr. Petrov. It was also possible that Mrs. Larson held something on Mr. Petrov, or threatened to break off the relationship, which would make him a suspect.

My mind turned in circles. The spiral of theories evaporated when I looked at the clock on the wall and realized it was time for my favorite television program, "Survivor."

*

Saturday came and with it an increased urgency to get justice for Mrs. Larson. I still felt ill when the thought of her violent murder crossed my mind, but time helped me to adjust to the truth of the matter. Jinx sat quietly alongside me in the Jeep with eyes glued to his phone as I drove toward the address I had acquired through an Internet search. Our destination, an old double story motel adjacent to the rail yard, lay in the seedy end of Falcon Ridge. A room on the ground floor occupied by one, Benjamin Black, aka Benny or Scar Cheek as we called him, featured highly amongst our morning's interests.

"Anyone who stays in a dump like this, doesn't like, earn much cheddar," said Jinx.

"He's only a stupid deckhand," I answered. Twaddle, jammed between the two of us, wagged his tail and looked undecided as to who should benefit from a heavy lick behind the ear.

Jinx chuckled. "Scar Cheek's a real dickhead."

I glanced at my watch. The trawlers didn't appear to work on weekends very often, so I hoped Scar Cheek would be at home. I hoped he might visit his cronies, or do something that could increase our understanding of his dirty world. This would be more of a stakeout to see what information we could glean. I parked the Jeep opposite the motel and we waited to see if anything would transpire.

Several cans of pop and a packet of potato chips later, our patience paid off as Scar Cheek came out of his room and clambered into an old derelict panel van. On the side panels, faded sign writing of a bakery business could still be seen and a huge plume of smoke billowed out of the exhaust as he turned the key in the ignition.

"Looks like we have ourselves a taker—he's ready to leave," I said.

"Be careful when you follow, dude. He mustn't like, see us."

"You throwing shade, Jinx? My dad's a cop and I know how to follow people."

Jinx laughed. "Just saying. I didn't like, mean anything by it. Bible."

Twaddle thought it his cue to chip in and gave a series of short coughs.

We followed the old van into the centre of town to a large vehicle repair shop and dealership, which sold late-model cars and took up several acres of real estate. Reardon Motors, advertised in large letters, appeared over the entrance.

Benny parked the van outside the building and walked into an office with a parcel under his arm.

"I wonder what he has in the parcel," I murmured.

"Let's go and see," said Jinx.

I parked the Jeep and ordered Twaddle to stay as we got out and walked across the road and into the building. My baseball cap, pulled low over my eyes, gave me a little bit of anonymity and I pulled up the collar of my windbreaker to hide as much of my identity as possible. We walked into the dealership and began to look at the new vehicles on the floor. There were two salespeople on duty, one busy with a client and the other sat at a desk making notes on a computer. Scar Cheek stood at the reception desk, waiting to get the attention of the receptionist.

A minute later she completed her phone call and smiled at him. "You want to see Mr. Reardon, Benny?"

"Yeah, he's expecting me," said Scar Cheek.

"Go in, then—don't keep him waiting."

Benny disappeared up a flight of stairs with the parcel still held under his one arm. We waited about a bit and checked out some of the cars and motor paraphernalia for sale, with our eyes on the entrance to the stairs.

After ten minutes or so Scar Cheek returned to the sales floor and stopped at the exit. We ducked down behind one of the vehicles so he wouldn't see us. I noticed he had something in his hands that took his attention. He was counting a wad of notes.

"Look at all that cheddar he's got in his hand," said Jinx.

"He must have got it from Mr. Reardon. I bet there was something illegal in that parcel. He doesn't have it with him anymore," I said.

Jinx agreed. "The dickhead's definitely like, up to something,"

Scar Cheek finished his count and a satisfied smile appeared on his face as he exited the building. We saw our opportunity and dashed out into the sunshine behind him with the hope of not being seeing. It was not to be. He must have heard something because he stopped, turned and stared back at us for a few seconds. I panicked and tried to hide behind Jinx, who also got a fright. I'd admit we acted like two frightened animals. He continued to stare at us for a long moment, then turned and walked off to his van.

We ran across the road and jumped into the Jeep. I performed a classic wheel spin on leaving the parking spot. Twaddle thought our hastiness had to be a game and he gave a few loud barks of approval.

"Let's go to the quarry," I shouted.

Jinx nodded and I took a shortcut through the industrial area. Ten minutes later we sat in our usual place on the ledge and checked our phones.

"Well, that was interesting," I said.

"Did you see the way he like, looked at us?"

"I hope he didn't recognize me from the boat-yard the other day."

"I doubt it, but I guess we should like, be careful in the future, dude"

"I guess. I think he's involved in something illegal and Mr. Reardon's a part of it."

"What are you going to do?" asked Jinx.

"I need to find something that belongs to Scar Cheek and touch it. More information about what he does, other than being a deckhand, might be revealed."

"That could like, be dangerous, dude."

"It could, and I don't want to be caught snooping around again, so you might be the better person to get something of his and bring it to me."

"Are you mad, Tess. What if he like, catches me?"

"Oh don't be a wanksta, Jinx. You just need to be careful, like your hero, James Bond—I have an idea."

His eyes lit up like a Christmas tree. There could be no greater hero for him than the fictional

Bond character. Jinx had seen every Bond movie ever made.

*

The following Tuesday afternoon I picked Jinx up and we headed for the quarry. He carried a brown paper bag in one hand and an apple in the other.

"I got what you needed," he said.

"What's in the bag?" I asked.

He opened the mouth of the bag and extended it for me to take a quick glance. Twaddle thought it to be something to eat and stuck his snout into the opening, only to receive a rebuke from both of us. He retreated with a hurt look in his eyes. Jinx extended the bag toward me again. I didn't want to get a fine for distracted driving so a brief glance was all that could be allowed—brown woolen cloth.

"You got hold of his toque?"

"I walked down to the boatyard yesterday and, like, went into the main office area. I like, saw it on a table in the corner."

"Where was Scar Cheek at the time?"

Jinx took a bite of his apple and spoke while he munched away. "Working on a stuck window or something—like, right there in front of me."

"Did he see you?"

"Um, Nope. Too busy." He checked his phone quickly.

"Well done, dude. I knew my plan would work and you'd come up with something."

Jinx beamed and managed a lop-sided grin. "Just like James Bond?"

I raised my eyebrows. I didn't know James Bond stole stuff but I let it lie.

With the Jeep parked, we walked to the lookout ledge and sat down. Jinx handed the bag to me and a wave of apprehension clouded my thoughts. Scar Cheek appeared to be a rough and unpredictable man with a devious nature. His very name —Benny Black—intimated a dark existence with unknown details, and to get mixed up with him in any way, may be dangerous for us.

I looked at the bag for a long moment before Jinx egged me on. "Come on...um, dude. What're you, like, waiting for?"

Twaddle wagged his tail and searched my eyes for a hint as to what this new game might be. I thought about the possible consequences for another few seconds before taking the plunge. With slow deliberation, I reached into the bag and took hold of the toque. The experience promised to be dramatic and I braced myself for it. Jinx waited with bated breath and Twaddle cocked his head to one side. What happened next took my breath away.

Ж

7

Unexpected Contraband

Darkness descended on me as the surroundings melted away. I remembered Jinx staring at my face with eyes that reflected concern for my safety and a fear of the unknown. I asked him to describe what he saw the last time I descended into a psychic trance and received the vague answer of uncertainty. As the light receded and darkness swirled in the form of black thunder clouds around my presence, I became aware of a foreboding, which clung to my soul like wet paper.

The air became sharp and clear. I looked out across a sea of dark, turbulent water and the immediate impression of a cold winter's day without sunshine greeted me. The trawler heaved over the crests and wallowed in the troughs of mountainous waves, etching out a path toward a light in the distant gloom. As we drew closer, I saw the light to be that of a buoy and the boat floated to a stop. A mechanical arm stretched out over the dark waters and snagged a line just below the surface. I'd seen this on telly when crab fishermen snag the lines which held the cages on the sea bottom.

A few minutes later a cage rose out of the water and a seaman grabbed its tether line. He swung the load over the boat's gunnel, and the winch deposited it onto the deck. I fully expected to see a whole bunch of crabs within the metal cage, but to my astonishment there appeared to be dozens of small containers, sealed and wrapped in plastic. The seaman opened the cage and turned it over to disgorge all the containers and they rolled onto the deck. He picked one up and lurched with the rolling of the sea toward the main cabin. I followed on behind him and he turned, as if aware of my presence. The soft light of the wheelhouse revealed his face and the scar across the cheek caught my attention. The immediate reaction was to hide my face, but he looked right through me and the realization came with some relief—he couldn't see me and had turned to close the cabin door.

I heard the captain's voice above the sound of the noisy engine. "Got the stuff, Benny?"

I looked to see who spoke and recognized the face of Kurt Larson. Scar Cheek broke away the plastic seal, pulled out the container and poured a white powder into the palm of his hand. He sniffed at it and then did a tongue-tip test.

"It's the right stuff all right, Captain. I'll pull up the rest of the cages and we can get back to port."

Benny Black poured the powder back into the container and placed it on the console. I knew what they were doing—smuggling drugs. Dad had spoken about an outbreak of drug-use in Falcon Ridge. Not that the town was free of drugs but there had been an unprecedented spike in over-doses and it became obvious a new or cheaper narcotic had become available. They were baffled as to who the supplier might be and now I knew—Mr. Larson. I wondered if Sam Petrov knew; maybe they were both involved. Now the disappearance of Mrs. Larson took on a whole new character.

I endured a frightening moment as Scar Cheek pushed straight by me to open the door and went out. Kurt Larson looked saddened by the event. He picked up the container and held it in his hand. I could barely hear his audible whisper. "Evelyn, oh my darling, Evelyn—why?"

I felt the sudden withdrawal of my presence back to the outside deck. The cold air swirled around my face as darkness swept me away, upward into the dark clouds above. The next thing I knew, Twaddle licked at my face and Jinx stood over me like the Statue of Liberty.

"Tessa; Tessa wake up, dude." I opened my eyes with great relief, to behold Jinx's terror-filled eyes.

I opened my eyes with great relief, to behold Jinx's terror-filled eyes.

"Geez, dude. You like, gave me such a fright. You passed out and fell onto the ground and I didn't know if you like, hurt yourself—Yolo."

"I'm fine, A little shaken, but okay. It was absolutely cray. I saw Scar Cheek and Mr. Petrov. They were pulling up drugs hidden in crab cages from the bottom of the sea."

"Drugs? You mean like heroin?"

"Yeah. Real hard drugs—white powder type drugs."

"Now we really like, have a reason for Mrs. Larson's disappearance."

"I didn't see anything which suggested that when in the wheelhouse. Mr. Larson looked at the drug container and whispered her name. He said her name twice—and then asked, 'why?'"

"Do you think I might have had something to do with like, her disappearance?"

I stroked Twaddle's head. "I'm not sure. But I would say he is a definite suspect in my mind. I have to somehow get my dad to suspect Larson of drug dealing to start with."

"I think I like, know a way."

"How?" I asked.

"Send like, an anonymous note to your dad and tell him to like, check the trawler for the drugs."

I thought about it for a moment. "I don't think it will work because the drugs may no longer be in the boat. What I saw may have taken place a while back. The last thing we must do is alert Mr. Larson that someone's onto his delinquent ways."

"Do you like, think Mr. Reardon at the car dealership might be involved too?" Jinx asked. That was actually a good point.

That was actually a good point.

"Come to think of it, you may be absolutely right, Jinx."

He beamed and looked up at the clouds. "Just how James Bond would like, think, eh?"

"You would have made a great buddy for Bond." I joked. He went red in the face as he usually did when paid a compliment.

"Bond is like, real sick, man," he gurgled. Jinx was one of the few who thought characters like Bond and Reacher were real people. Though the truth might be a revelation for him, I didn't feel I should be the one to burst his bubble.

"That parcel Scar Cheek delivered to Reardon was about the right size to be one of those drug canisters I saw."

"Another like, possible suspect in Mrs. Larson's disappearance."

"I think we're actually getting somewhere, at last, dude—woot."

This time he lifted his chin, gazed up at the sky and let out a clucking sound that drew Twaddle's attention. I laughed, gave Jinx's ankle a kick and the game started. We jumped up, raced around the bushes and ducked behind trees, much to the pit bull's joy. It almost ended in tragedy when Twaddle got too close to the ledge in a tug-of-war with Jinx and before we could do anything the dog slipped over the edge and dropped into the lake below.

Jinx and I jerked out of our high-spirited fun and peered over the ledge with concern. Twaddle landed in the water, sinking out of sight with only a trail of bubbles popping up to the surface to mark his position. A few seconds later, his head broke the surface and he swam toward the wall of rock.

I knew he could never get out there so both Jinx and I ran down the path to the small beach of sand on the west side of the quarry and called him to swim in our direction. He turned and swam with powerful strokes toward our position and several minutes later managed to exit the lake. After a good shake, he seemed, apart from hurt pride, none the worse for his experience.

"We had better get going," I said. "Twaddle's had enough fun for one day."

I dropped Jinx off at his house and drove home. Twaddle, in full recovery of his escapade, stood on the jeeps back seat and barked at everyone we passed. My mind became absorbed with the new details we had uncovered and when I pulled up in the driveway Miss Bennet's car blocked my usual space. I wondered why she had come to visit.

*

I walked into the sitting room to find dad and Miss Bennett in earnest discussion. They broke off the conversation and looked up at me as I entered the room.

"Ah...home at last. Miss Bennett has come to invite us to a gathering of her students and parents at the Town Hall. Apparently, there are changes to some of the subjects being proposed by Central Education and she needs our opinion."

I must have seemed a little surprised and confessed that I hoped she had come to invite us to a barbecue or something.

"Why us? I'm in my final year, so any change to the curriculum won't affect me," I said.

Miss Bennett smiled and looked at my dad. They had obviously discussed the point before my arrival. "It will be helpful for all students and parents involved in private tuition to give their opinion so that the future changes can be assessed," said dad.

I couldn't argue with the logic. "Sounds fine to me—when?"

"Tomorrow night at 7:00. We can eat out and you won't have to cook."

"Great," I said. I hoped there might be more to the invitation. I always felt Miss Bennett would be a good match for my dad, despite his notion of being too old for her. I had often wanted to invite her for dinner but he declined every time for indistinct reasons. I would have thought five years would be enough time for him to get over mom's death.

"Would you like a drink....err, Miss Bennett?" dad ventured.

"Please call me Margaret, sheriff," she replied. "What do you have?"

"And I'm Luke." He called a list of drinks off the top of his head and turned to me. "Please get us some ice, cupcake."

She asked for a sherry. He pulled out a bottle of KWV and a small glass and then poured himself a whiskey. I brought the ice.

"Can I get you something, sweetheart?"

Emboldened by Miss Bennett's presence, I asked for some sherry. "Nice try, cupcake," said my dad. "I meant a pop or something like that."

I shrugged and let it pass. Maybe next year when I turned nineteen. We sat for another hour and made small talk. At 6:30, Miss Bennett took her leave and I cleared the empty glasses away. Time to begin prep for dinner.

"She's nice, isn't she?" I asked.

Dad continued to read his magazine. "Who, honey?"

"You know very well who," I said. "Margaret."

"Oh, yeah, she seems cool."

"You should get to know her better. I think she likes you."

Tessa—we've talked about this before. Just drop it."

"You're just avoiding getting on with your life." My tone came across a little more bitter than intended. "It's time you let your hair down a bit."

He glared at me and put the magazine down. "I'm going to have a shower. Call me when dinner's ready." He stalked off in the direction of the bathroom.

"You're so freakin' stubborn," I mumbled.

Ж

8

A Chat at Breakfast

I awoke the next morning with Sheba lying against my cheek and for a moment thought I'd gone to sleep with the imitation fur scarf dad gave me for Christmas wrapped around my neck. I pushed her away so I could breathe; she meowed, wagged her tail and stuck out a paw to dab at my cheek in annoyance. The memory of the previous day's revelation returned to spark a range of options available for action and as the sun's rays peeked in through the window, I decided to get up and start breakfast. The Tamburrino family had always been early risers due mainly to dad's job as sheriff, but I have never been one to lie in.

The smell of scrambled eggs greeted me. Dad, in an effort to do his bit, had beaten me to it and a quick peek into the pan revealed a congealed mess of yellow, which turned my stomach a little. I hated hurting his feelings when he had gone out of his way to do a good thing, so I made toast and dished up a sparse helping of the egg. The coffee was usually okay—not much he can mess up there and with breakfast in hand, I marched into the dining room. Dad sat with an empty plate and half-full mug of coffee, reading the morning newspaper.

"Morning, cupcake. Sleep well?"

"Like a log," I said.

I could see the front page of the news—a headline caught my eye:

A spike in drug use plagues east end of town.

"I see drugs are on the increase."

He dropped the paper and peered over the top of a page at me. "Yes, we've taken more than the usual number of users into custody and there has been a spike in overdoses. No one is saying where they got the drugs from—there appears to be a new supplier in town."

"Could it be coming in by sea, from the mainland?" I thought I would throw it out there.

"It's possible. With two dozen fishing businesses on the island, it would mean checking every vessel that comes and goes each day and we just don't have the resources to do that."

"What other possible avenues are available?"

"The airport, the container business, and the ferry. Someone could also be making the drug locally."

I drank my coffee and let him finish.

"A home-lab is quite probable, perhaps even more so than an import situation. I'm sure a lead will come in soon to provide us with more substantial clues," he said.

His expectations were in line with much of his receipt of clues, many of which, in the past, came out of the blue—compliments of my psychic gift. I hoped he wasn't relaxing in such hope because I may not always be able to come through. This time, however, there had to be a way to do it. Justice for Evelyn Larson brooded with constant insistence at the back of my mind.

Dad put down his empty mug and stood. "I have to get to work. Are you doing anything this afternoon after your tuition?"

I shook my head. "Not that I can think of—why?"

"Don't forget we have that thing with your tutor at the city hall tonight."

"You mean Margaret?"

"Ah...yes." He blushed a little and my hopes soared.

"I haven't forgotten. We can eat early."

He hesitated. "Actually, I've invited her to have a bite to eat with us after the meeting—we'll be going to Dino's"

"Bravo, dad. That's perf. Glad to see you're taking the bull by the horns."

"As you said, cupcake. I ain't getting any younger."

"It's on fleek, dad. I really like her."

"I'm not promising anything," he said.

I laughed as he came around the table to kiss me goodbye.

It was funny but later as my tuition wore on I couldn't help seeing Margaret Bennett in a new light.

*

After Miss Bennett left I had time to think about the possible actions available with regards to Mr. Larson and his drug business. One thought did come to mind: I needed to establish when they took trips to pick up the drugs and also when Scar Cheek made his drop to Reardon's dealership. It made sense that the two events would follow each other as a matter of course. Saturday appeared to be the day for drop-off; therefore, Friday might well be the day they would go out to the crab cages. Reardon may not be the only client, but that was beside the point.

To simply expose the drug business would not solve the murder of Mrs. Larson but it may provide my dad with a group of suspects and a prime motive. It seemed doubtful Scar Cheek would have murdered Mrs. Larson for some reason of his own. He more than likely would have been doing someone else's dirty work for them. Without a body, the only crime possible was foul play in Mrs. Larson's disappearance and no one could be convicted of her murder because, as far as anyone knew, no murder had been committed. At some point, I needed to work out who gave Benny Black his orders, and then see what could be gleaned through my psychic ability. I may get lucky and see where they dumped the body. I did have an idea it would be somewhere near the crab-traps due to the possibility of a combined effort to save fuel.

I remembered seeing a large wall chart of the fishing areas in the boatyard office. An idea spawned in my head, to study it and see where the prime fishing spots were, but it would mean going there again. My horror of bumping into Scar Cheek discouraged the idea some, however, it had to be done. Jinx had an after-school function, so I decided to do it on my own. The possibility of seeing Petrov also scared me. He more than likely would recognize my face from our confrontation at the Larson residence.

It took another hour of building up the courage to go to the boatyard. Twenty minutes after leaving home, Twaddle and I arrived in the Jeep and parked outside the gate. I didn't want Twaddle to accompany me into the office in case Petrov was there and saw him. He straightened up his ears when I told him to stay in the Jeep and his large, greenish-yellow eyes looked soulfully back at me as if to ask why. A quick look at the wharf told me the trawlers were both out on the water. This meant both Kurt Larson and Sam Petrov would not be in the office. I walked toward the building with much trepidation. An old man busied himself behind the counter with something but took no notice of me as I walked across the open customer space to the wall chart.

Not understanding much about nautical charts, I stared at it for a long while, conscious of the old man at the counter. I noticed a few circles, drawn with a pencil, around a few of the areas with "crab cages" written next to them. I took out my phone and after checking on the old guy clicked off two photos. Oblivious of my presence, he continued to work on something behind the counter. I couldn't believe my luck.

There were numbers written down next to the pencil-drawn circles and I gathered these would be the latitudes and longitudes involved with the positioning of the cages. There were five different positions throughout the entire area of the strait between our island and the mainland. This information would help someone with knowledge of such things to know where to find the drugs. How this information would get into police hands would be another story.

I left the office without the old man having the slightest clue I was there. Twaddle gave two short coughs, happy to see me and pulled the upper lip thing. We sped off in the direction of home with the notion of finally getting somewhere with the case.

I arrived home and saved the photos to my laptop. The information would remain as background until I could figure out how to make it useful. Dad arrived just before five and we got ready for the evening out. I showered, dressed and waited for him to present himself for inspection. He needed to look his best and I so wanted him to latch onto Miss Bennett. It was my belief he had been a bachelor for long enough and it certainly didn't bother me if he had someone else in his life. I loved my dad, but I wasn't going to cook for him for the rest of my days. No way.

The meeting in the town hall went off well and Miss Bennett outlined the changes in the curriculum to the parents of the children involved in her private tutoring program. The other students were kids, with just two of us in the final year. I listened with half an ear, as the changes would not affect me, all the while allowing my mind to roam over the Larson case details. At 8:00, Miss Bennett ended her explanations and the others left while dad and I waited for her to pack up her laptop and books.

We drove in separate vehicles to Dino's and after arrival took up our reservation. My nerves acted up a little for my dad's sake, and perspiration broke out on my brow as we took our seats and placed orders. I could see Miss Bennett also felt nervous as she glanced at me and then at my dad and I hoped he would initiate some conversation, but he sat there with a mouth full of teeth.

Miss Bennett turned to me for comfort. "How are you getting along, Tess?"

"Just fine," I said.

"Have you decided what you're going to do next year?"

"Not really—college, I guess." I kicked my dad's leg under the table and saw him stiffen. For a second he stared at me and then got the message.

"I think Tess will make a fine lawyer," he said.

Miss Bennett turned back to him. "And why do you say that, Luke?"

"Because she's stubborn and can argue the living daylights out of any subject."

We all laughed and the ice was broken.

At that moment a familiar face entered the restaurant. I nearly did a double take—Mr. Larson. On his arm was a younger woman, not very attractive, but then the man himself did not inspire an attraction. Not to me, anyway. I looked at dad and could see the cogs turning in his mind. Larson's wife had been missing for one week and he already looked to a new relationship. Strange.

Ж

9

Mr. Larson

Our dinner outing went well until Mr. Larson entered the restaurant with the strange woman on his arm. My thoughts dissolved into turmoil and for me, he became the chief suspect in the disappearance of his wife, Evelyn. As much as I tried to make intelligent conversation at the table, my mind became consumed by speculation as to how his wife may have incurred his wrath. Her affair with Sam Petrov climbed to the top of my list. Maybe I watched too many movies, but many jealous spouses kill an unfaithful partner or the partner's lover.

My dad also became a little distracted at first, but he appeared to enjoy the attention Miss Bennett gave him and the evening wore on for another hour before we called it a night. On the way home, I ventured the question uppermost in my mind.

"Did you see Mr. Larson?"

"Sure did, cupcake."

"He's seeing someone else and it's only been a week," I complained.

"I know, sweetheart, but don't jump to conclusions."

"But, dad, it's too soon after his wife's disappearance. He must have wanted to get rid of her."

"As I said, Tessa. Don't jump to conclusions—there may be an acceptable reason for it."

I wanted to tell him about my vision of Sam Petrov and Mrs. Larson's affair but caught myself just in time. Being a strong-willed person it's difficult to quell the instinct for clarity and I had to bite my tongue.

"Are you going to look into it?" I asked.

"I certainly will, sweetheart, now please drop the issue. I know you want justice for Mrs. Larson, but don't get yourself tied in a knot because of it."

I let it go at that. I didn't want to raise his suspicions. We drove home in silence from there on, each absorbed with our own thoughts. In contemplation of the issue, a thought came to me—there had to be evidence of the illicit love affair. Two people cannot carry on a relationship in total secrecy unless they're ghosts. Maybe Mrs. Larson kept a diary. The details in the file my dad left on the dining room table came to mind: the police had found a cell phone on the counter next to her handbag. The phone had no suspicious texts or phone numbers which were out of the scope of her normal relationships. They had questioned Kurt Larson extensively, but no connection with the disappearance had been made to Sam Petrov.

The thought of a diary intrigued me, but where would she keep such a record? Certainly not where anyone, her husband, in particular, would find it. The revelation of Evelyn's murder came forcibly back to me and I knew there might be a way I could get her to reveal further clues. It would entail touching a very personal, intimate object or possession, a much more recent photo, perhaps. I did not, however, want to go back to the Larson residence. Maybe I could convince Jinx to do it. Somewhere in those boxes, or in the house, lay a secret to be revealed and I felt desperate to find it.

We arrived home and both made for our beds. Before donning my favorite PJ's, I stood at the mirror to survey myself as I usually did. The leg stump looked ugly and unnatural, but everything else appeared normal. Shapely hips and glutes, boobs fully developed, a narrow waist and a flat stomach. What more could a teenage girl ask for? Except for that stupid stump, of course. I said what I always say: "You're one bad-assed beauty, Tessa."

Feeling suitably complimented, I jumped into bed. Sheba took up her position against the small of my back and Twaddle, next to my good leg. After checking my phone for a few minutes, I turned the light out and sleep took me away to the land of dreams.

*

Miss Bennett arrived for the morning's tutorship, which began with classical Greek History and ended with Physics and chemistry. My mind still grappled with the previous evening's events at the restaurant and I found it difficult to concentrate. When Miss Bennett left, I phoned Jinx's cell. Fortunately, he was on a break and answered immediately.

I explained what had taken place the previous evening. "You've got to help me get some more information," I demanded.

"Like what, dude?"

"I need a very recent, personal item of Mrs. Larson's. She must have kept stuff at her office, behind the counter, where she worked."

"You want me to like, go back there and find something?" asked Jinx.

"Please dude—just for little, old me. Put your James Bond cap on."

I knew if I made the connection to Bond, he would agree.

"I guess. There's nothing Bond can't do."

"Mr. Larson appears to have employed an old guy to work behind the counter. I guess he needed to get back to his trawler. The old guy should go off to the toilet occasionally so if you wait outside at the entrance, where he can't see you, you may get a chance to sneak in and have a look."

"It's like, a big risk. What if Scar Cheek is like, around?"

"Bond would know exactly what to do," I said. I had a tone of voice—like velvet when I wanted Jinx to do something for me. It worked every time.

"S'true. Just like in 'Spectre,' remember?"

"How could I ever forget that movie?" I lied.

We talked about James Bond movies for another five minutes until the school bell ended their break-time.

"So, you'll do it this afternoon? I'll pick you up after school."

"Could be a bit like, really awks, but if Bond could do it so can I."

With the issue settled I waited for 3:00 p.m. and then drove to Jinx's home with Twaddle in command of the passenger seat.

*

I parked the Jeep near the entrance to the boatyard. Both trawlers were gone from the wharf, which assured us we should not be bumping into Petrov, Larson or Scar Cheek. Two boat-builders, busy with various repair jobs in the yard, took no notice of us as we scampered across the open drive-in area to the office building. Jinx stood at the wall adjacent to the counter, where some sailing magazines lay while I sauntered over to a shelf containing numerous model sailboats on sale. The old man looked up and smiled at me. "Looking for something special?" he asked.

I pointed to one of the models. "I'm interested in this one. It would look great in our sitting room."

He left the counter and strutted over to me. Out of the corner of my eye, I saw Jinx move in behind the counter. The old man picked the model sailboat up and turned it around to give me a better look.

"It's a classic single hull made by Perini Navi's Reila, a sailing super yacht, and a real beauty."

He seemed to know a lot about yachts, so I pumped him for more information.

"Is it an exact replica?"

He warmed to the theme. "It's exact in every detail and if you can afford the price, it's a collector's prize. There are only a few of them in the world."

I cast my eye beyond the old man's shoulder and saw Jinx come out from behind the counter.

"How much does it sell for?"

"Fifteen hundred and sixty-five dollars."

I screwed up my nose and gave him a wistful look. "I'm afraid that's a bit too rich for me. I have to get going—thanks for the information," I said.

Jinx nodded at me from the doorway and I felt elated, hopeful we had what I needed. The old guy seemed a little put out as I turned and walked to the door. He stared at me for a long while as Jinx and I beat a retreat to the boatyard entrance. We jumped up into the Jeep, much to Twaddle's delight, and raced off down the road. Jinx put his head back and laughed out aloud.

"Just as Bond would have like, done."

"You're a true 007, Jinx. Bond would have been proud of you. Now, what did you find?"

He opened his hand and revealed a lipstick container. My hopes soared. Mrs. Larson would have last used her lipstick on the day she disappeared. I couldn't hope for anything better.

"You're a genius, Jinx."

"Yea, I know. It's like, in my blood."

I made for the old quarry, parked the Jeep and we assumed our usual place on the ledge. The afternoon, a little cool sported a light breeze and we huddled together with Twaddle between us, to coax out as much warmth as possible. I felt a twinge of nervous apprehension when I asked Jinx to hand me the lipstick container. A moment of truth awaited me and hope for Mrs. Larson's justice hung in the balance.

Jinx dug the container out of his pocket and stretched around Twaddle to hand it to me. Twaddle, thinking it was meant for him, sniffed at Jinx's hand and tried to snatch it with his teeth, but I quickly grabbed it. The moments that followed were as equally dramatic as the previous psychic incursions.

*

I had never been able to establish how this worked. Whether science played a part, or if it was an interfacing of minds with a spirit world that lies beyond our natural realm, I couldn't tell. All I knew was that it was real, and very scary, enough to have me shaking all over for an hour or so afterward.

The moment my fingers touched the lipstick canister, a defocus of my surroundings occurred and a new world transitioned through a misty swirl of shadows and dark forms. When the transition completed, I found myself sitting on a bench, surrounded by beautiful plants and bushes. The deep green color of the grass lawn and the exotic flowers that grew in the garden impressed me as I admired the extensive beauty of my surroundings. Something on the bench beside me caught my attention.

I stretched out a hand to lift it into view and saw a small flat wooden box wrapped in clear plastic appear. I glanced at my other hand and in it rested a gardening trowel. I assumed with an immediate understanding I was seeing the scene before me through Mrs. Larson's eyes, and for a long moment, we sat there in observance of the garden's beauty. The sun's warmth seeped through the vision into my being. With a sudden lurch, we stood and moved toward the garden bed, to the base of a lilac bush and knelt down to the ground. Miss Bennett covered many types of flowers and exotic bushes in a one-time lesson in home economics and I recognized the lilacs. I felt the digging motion of Mrs. Larson's right hand and understood she wanted to bury the wooden box in a shallow hole. The other hand moved to drop the box into its grave and the motion of the trowel as she covered the hole over with the loose soil.

Another sensation invaded my senses and my eyes blurred. Mrs. Larson was crying. I tried to extend my vision to take in more of the surroundings, which resulted in the same view of the garden, through the blur of her tears. All the colors ran into each other. With a sudden shift of perspective, the garden and the bench retreated into the dark swirl of shadow and I knew the vision had come to an end. The sounds of the quarry's birdlife grew loud in my ears and I opened my eyes to find myself lying on my back with Twaddle and Jinx staring at me like two expectant mothers.

The look of relief on Jinx's face made me chuckle.

"Cripes, dude. I hate it when you do this. I don't know if you're like, dead or alive. Where do you go to?"

Twaddle gave his two cough-like barks in approval and I sat up. "I go to wherever the object takes me. Don't ask how this happens because I can't explain it."

"What did you see?"

I told him what I had seen. "I'm just at a loss as to where this garden might be. I don't recall there being anything like it in the Larson's yard."

Jinx wiped his nose with the back of a hand. "I...um, think I might know."

Ж

10

The Botanical Gardens

I stared at him for a full second. He really did seem to have a Bond-like way of working things out. I almost found myself believing in his self-imposed notion of being linked with the fictional super spy.

"Where do you think it might be?" I asked.

"As you like, described the grass it sounds like the botanical garden lawns to me."

"You know about the Falcon Ridge botanical gardens? Have you been there?"

"Um...no, but we saw, like a short film show last—week like, during one of our lessons."

It was one place I'd never been. "We should go there right away and see if we can find the place where Mrs. Larson buried the box."

"You have to like, pay to get in."

That took the wind out of my sails. "How much?"

"About twelve bucks."

"Where am I going to get that sort of cheddar?"

"I'm sure we could like, find a way in."

"You learn that from the guys at school?" I asked.

"We never pay for anything when there's like, another way."

I hated to break the law. My dad was the sheriff of Falcon Ridge and if I were to be caught it would reflect badly on us.

"I would rather pay. I have a little money saved —didn't expect to use it on something like this, though."

"Suit yourself, dude."

I decided to appeal to his ego. "You've done your share, Jinxie. You must remember to give Mr. Bond my best."

He beamed at me. "You're welcome, dude."

We left the quarry and I drove Jinx home.

*

The following morning I left Twaddle, much to his chagrin, drove to the botanical gardens and paid for an entrance ticket. My parents, to my knowledge, had never visited the gardens because my dad's work always kept him so busy. Mom also never bothered much with our garden and I guess their interests lay elsewhere. I walked down the main pathway and wondered where I would find the place of interest. A gardener passed me with a barrow full of soil and I popped the question.

"Where would I be able to see lilacs in bloom?"

The gardener pointed to a path leading off the main one. "Just take that path and when you come over the crest of that rise, the lilacs are growing amongst a group of bushes on your left."

I thanked her and walked toward the rise of the hillock that hid the rest of the gardens from view. A few minutes late I crested the hill and marveled at the beautiful lush, green lawns sprawling across a wide area of ground. My heart lurched when I saw the bench—identical to the one in my vision. There, at the edge of the lawn in the garden, grew the lilac bushes. I felt a lurch in my stomach and almost brought up my breakfast. As I limped up to the bench and sat down I could almost sense the dark, swirling shadows around me, threatening to snatch away the scene before me.

The feeling passed and I looked around to see if anyone else shared the area with me. The gardens, it would seem, received their greatest amount of visitors on the weekends and the place appeared deserted. I moved toward the lilac bush closest to me and knelt down to search for the exact area where Mrs. Larson had dug the shallow hole. Why had she chosen this place to bury it? Not sure. I dug the loose soil away with my bare hands and at about a depth of six inches, I felt the box. The plastic wrap had protected the wood from the elements and I lifted it out of the hole. I pushed back the soil and smoothed it over. Another look around confirmed the continued absence of any other people so I straightened up, moved back to the bench and took a seat.

The wrap came off easily. The box appeared to have been constructed for jewelry, with an ornate lid and body, made mostly of a light wood. The small golden clasp unclipped with ease and I opened the lid, interested to see the contents—a wad of folded papers tied up with a thin pink ribbon and a cell phone. The folded papers appeared to be notes or letters. A silver chain with a heart-shaped container with a clasp glinted in the overhead sunlight and I lifted it clear of the box to have a better look. The clip gave some trouble, but when I managed to open the container, a tiny picture on each side came to light. I gasped. They were photos of Mrs. Larson and Sam Petrov. A quick look at one of the notes, written in a rough scrawl and signed "Sam" confirmed my suspicions.

My psychic gift proved true with respect to their affair and therefore the murder would also be true. At least I had some proof, which could start the ball rolling. I stood to leave, but a voice from behind almost caused me to drop the box.

"Enjoying the scenery?"

I went cold all over in recognition of the voice—the man who accosted me in the Larson's yard and whom Twaddle had bitten—Sam Petrov. His olive skin, deeply tanned by the sun made him look a lot younger than his photo and his eyes, narrowed to mere slits, held mine with a frightening intensity. I wanted to scream, but no sound came from my mouth. My body felt numb with fear and perspiration broke out on my brow.

He reached out a hand. "I'll take that box you're holding."

I found my voice at last. "No you can't—it belongs to me."

"I know who you are," he said. "You and that damn dog of yours caused me a bit of a problem in the Larson's yard the other day. I'm prepared to overlook that if you give me the box."

I remained silent and held his gaze. He tilted his head to one side.

"What I don't know is how you knew about this box buried here by the lilacs, and why you were sneaking around the boatyard yesterday."

I clutched the box to my breast and looked him straight in the eye. "It's none of your business."

"Oh, but it is. There are letters in that box which belong to me."

I looked beyond his shoulder and saw the gardener standing at the crest of the hill. She had a man with her and they were discussing something to do with the gardens near the path.

Sam Petrov's shoulders slumped and he dropped his chin. "I didn't have anything to do with her disappearance, you know."

His words shocked me to the core and I didn't know what to say, then it occurred to me— he didn't appear to know she was dead. Only the murderer would know. Scar Cheek worked on Kurt Larson's boat and I knew he had done the deed, but did he kill her without his boss's knowledge? My mind leaped back to the vision of Kurt Larson in the trawler when he grabbed the canister of drugs and whispered his anguish over Evelyn's disappearance. He seemed genuinely grieved.

Petrov's voice cut into my thoughts. "The letters in that box are from me to her—they're love letters. We were having an affair. She decided to call it off as things had become too dangerous. Kurt was on the verge of finding out."

"Why are you telling me this?" I stammered.

"I know you are the sheriff's daughter and somehow you've managed to cotton on to the fact that Evelyn Larson and I were lovers. It's not news I would like to have shouted out to the world and I'm not proud of the fact."

I could not reveal what I knew. If Petrov didn't murder her, it could only have been on Kurt Larson's order—or Scar Cheek had committed the murder due to some reason yet to be revealed. I felt conflicted and a little confused.

"You'll have to tell the police about it. They are bound to find out sooner or later," I said.

His chin sank even lower and he seemed quite ashamed. I saw a tear slip out of an eye and his voice shook with emotion. "I know I have to do that. If you give me the box I will promise to do it. I was just so scared because Evelyn's husband, Kurt, doesn't know anything about the affair."

Emboldened by his sudden change of attitude I ventured, "Do you think he may have had something to do with her disappearance?"

"Who, Kurt?" he asked. "I don't know—it's a possibility, but I doubt it. If he knew he would probably have killed me by now." He held out his hand again. "Please..."

I handed the box over, not knowing if it was the right thing to do. He stood for a while and looked at it before he gave me a weak smile, turned and started to walk back up the path.

My heart nearly stopped beating as I contemplated the entire confrontation. Had I done the right thing? The waters, if murky before, now seemed like mud.

"Remember your promise, Mr. Petrov," I shouted.

He raised a hand in an acknowledgment without turning around and somehow I knew he would go to the police.

I sat down on the bench to catch my breath. When I thought about it, having him go to the police instead of the evidence anonymously being left for my dad to find, worked out better for me in the long run. I still needed to find a way to expose Scar Cheek—he was the one who had actual blood on his hands. I still couldn't believe he killed her for his own reasons. After a few more minutes of recuperation, it became evident my nerve had sufficiently recovered to leave the gardens.

The drive back home gave me more time to think about the situation and I became convinced Kurt Larson had everything to do with his wife's demise. Perhaps she had found out about his drug dealings and threatened to report it. Perhaps he found out about her affair with Sam Petrov, or perhaps Scar Cheek acted on his own accord. All these theories coalesced into a melting pot of possibilities, and by the time I arrived home, my mind wanted to go on strike.

My dad arrived an hour later to a fully prepared meal and we sat down to eat.

"What did you do today, cupcake?"

"Nothing much. I went to the botanical gardens."

He looked at me with amusement. "You went to the gardens, why?"

"I've taken a sudden interest in flowers."

"Oh—any particular type?"

"Lilacs," I said.

He smiled. "You really surprise me sometimes, sweetheart."

"Yeah, I'm not just a pretty face."

Dad's cell phone rang and he reached for it. I could hear the intensity of the voice on the other side of the conversation as his eyes grew bigger and rounder.

"He what? When?"

The voice blared indistinctly again. Dad's eyes moved with a slow deliberation to focus on me and I knew, somehow, I was in trouble.

"Okay Blair—keep a lid on it for now. Tell him to go home and chill. I'll read his statement and contact him in the morning."

Dad put the phone down and stared at me. "Sam Petrov just walked into the office and gave a statement. He said you convinced him to do it. Would you like to explain, Tessa?"

ЖК

11

Almost Busted

I could feel my cheeks turning crimson. I must be naive because the thought of Sam Petrov giving the details of our conversation away did not occur to me. The question throbbed in my skull—should I tell my dad the truth? After several moments of hesitation, I opened my mouth but no words came out.

"Well? What do you have to say, young lady?" The impatience in his voice showed.

"I ran into him at the botanical garden today," I said.

Dad stared at me and I could see doubt written all over his face. "You met with him in the gardens? How did you know about his story?"

I gathered my wits and realized I couldn't tell him the whole truth, so a half-truth would have to do. "I found a small box beneath a lilac bush while walking through a section of the gardens and it happened to belong to Mrs. Larson, although I didn't know it at the time. Mr. Petrov happened on the scene as I was about to open the box and asked me to hand it over, but I refused."

"He happened to arrive right at the moment you found it under a lilac bush? That's quite a co-incidence, Tessa."

"I guess," I said. "He told me the box belonged to Mrs. Larson and that she must have dropped it." I hated lying to my dad, after all, he was the chief of police in Falcon Ridge. One thing in my favor rested in the fact of the box's initial discovery— Sam Petrov had not asked me how I came about it. Emboldened by this fact I continued my explanation.

"I took a peek at the contents and saw it contained some love letters. He told me he and Mrs. Larson had been involved in an affair but had been afraid to tell the police because he didn't want Kurt Larson to know about it."

Dad's eyes glazed over a bit as he thought about the implications and I could see the cloud of doubt lift a fraction.

"What I don't understand is the timing of all this. You decided today, you would go to the gardens, a place in which you have never shown any interest before, and it happens to be the exact time he is in the same place. You find a small box with letters in it and he comes across you at that exact moment. Is there something you're not telling me?"

I could almost see the cogs turning like well-oiled gears and I wanted to tell him the full truth, but again, his opinion of psychics constrained the notion.

"I know it seems like a real coincidence to you, dad, but that's how it happened. He knew I was your daughter and decided to come clean in case I mentioned the meeting. I did tell him you would find out in the end and it would be better for him to tell you, rather sooner than later."

Dad rubbed his chin—the aura of doubt hung around him like a mist. I would stick to this story, however. No one else other than Jinx knew about my strange abilities, and I wanted to keep it that way.

Dad held my gaze for a few more moments and then shrugged. "If what you say is true, then I guess you did a good thing. This opens up a new line of investigation, however, and does point a finger at Mr. Larson."

I experienced a sensation of relief. My dad still had questions but at least, for the moment, the pendulum of suspicion had swung in the right direction—toward Kurt Larson.

"Did you find out who Mr. Larson was with at the restaurant, the other night?" I asked.

He nodded. "She happens to be his sister and had arrived from the mainland that morning."

This bit of information took the wind out of my sails and all I could muster was a disappointed, "I see."

I decided to beat a hasty retreat to my bedroom and made an excuse to leave the table. The news regarding Kurt Larson's female acquaintance, being his sister and not a fling, dampened my ardor somewhat. It still didn't let him off the hook, however. Twaddle and Sheba joined me on the bed where the usual face-off between them took place. Sheba bristled like a wire brush while Twaddle grinned at her in an attempt to turn the whole confrontation into a game.

I picked up my phone and went to my facebook page to see if there were any messages from Bree or Jan, then did a search on the Internet for Sam Petrov. I wanted to know more about him because it would appear I had, to some extent, misjudged his persona. Not a great deal of information came out of the search but to my surprise, I learned he had a degree in business management. That explained his business affiliation with Kurt Larson, as a part owner in the boatyard. He captained one of the trawlers, the "Misty Maiden," and had grown up involved in his father's fishing business until hard times shut them down. He had been a co-director in the boatyard for five years. Petrov's wife, Becky, was a homemaker and looked after their two young children.

Not a great deal of information to go by but the more I thought about it, despite the affair with Mrs. Larson, Sam Petrov appeared to be an honest guy. More and more the feeling that Kurt Larson could have found out about his wife's infidelity and had her murdered in a fit of rage, seemed a reasonable theory. Perhaps Petrov was in danger of following a similar fate. This frightened me and I lay thinking about it long after lights-out. Sam Petrov may make a good ally in my quest to find Evelyn Larson's real murderer. Benny Black might be the key to exposing Kurt Larson but without proof of the crime, I couldn't think of where to start. Would it be wise to take Petrov into my confidence or might he still be a suspect? I felt torn and only managed to fall asleep in the early hours of the morning.

Dad did not say much at breakfast and I concluded he had a lot on his mind with the latest turn of events. He left with a cursory peck on my cheek and I felt bad at having led him astray the previous evening. Miss Bennett arrived at the usual time and we started lessons, with me going through the motions for most of the morning. My mind strayed back to Sam Petrov and whether I should speak to him. He may not be adverse to my psychic insights and I certainly needed help in finding a way to prove Scar Cheek's and possibly Kurt Larson's complicity. Then an idea came to me. It seemed probable Petrov did not know about the crab-trap drug scenario. I had the photo of the coordinates on my phone and he would be able to read them. Perhaps if we could prove Kurt Larson's involvement it would be possible to swing the police's investigation in a new direction. The more I thought about it the more the idea took hold.

By the time Miss Bennet left at 11:00 am this course of action became very plausible and only one thought plagued me—one more person would know about my abilities. This presented a scary set of possibilities and I felt threatened by it. I would swear him to secrecy. If he accepted the fact that I could see things beyond the normal range of human perception, then he should also accept my vision of the drug stash. With this mindset, I picked up Sam's cell number from the photocopy of the original detail sheet my dad had brought home and made the call. As I waited for him to answer, all sorts of apprehensive questions crossed my mind. I was about to cancel the call when his voice cut through my imaginations.

"Sam, here."

I hesitated. "Um...Mr. Petrov, it's Tessa Tamburrino, the girl you met in the botanical gardens yesterday."

"I did as you asked." He sounded a bit defensive.

"I know. My dad told me last night. I felt I owed you an explanation."

"An explanation? About what?"

"About how I knew the box was there. I would like to talk to you, if I may," I said.

"This isn't some type of a police trap is it?"

"No, sir. I promise you, my dad knows nothing about this. There are certain things I can't tell him...about how I know things. He wouldn't understand, but I thought you might."

A short silence followed then he said, "Okay, I'm listening."

"I don't want to talk on the phone. Can I meet you at Harvey's, the coffee shop on Eagle's Nest road?"

"What time? I have to take my boat out at 3:30."

"I'll see you there at 2:00."

*

I walked into Harvey's Coffee Shop at 2:05 p.m. and saw Sam sitting in the back corner with a cup of coffee in hand. He gave me an appraising glance and I felt self-conscious as his stare raked my body from head to foot. He stood as I approached and waited for me to reach the table before he took his chair again.

"Can I get you a cup of coffee?" he asked.

I nodded. "With cream and sugar," I said. He stepped over to the counter and placed the order, which took a minute to fill and then he walked back, placing the mug in front of me as he sat.

We contemplated each other. He was not bad looking and a little younger than his partner, Kurt Larson. His eyes were pale blue and the blond hair covered his ears, to dovetail at the back of his neck and his hands were rough at the fingertips. He seemed uneasy.

"So, Tessa. We meet again. Come to think of it I realize now that I never did get an explanation of how you knew about the box. I think I was so shocked to see it in your hands and I just wanted it back. Did you see her bury it?"

"No. I have had little to do with Mrs. Larson since my days as a girl guide."

"How did you find out then?"

I gathered my thoughts. "I have a gift," I said. I told him about the accident that took my mom's life and nearly my own—how I discovered my new talent and what I had seen regarding the burying of the box. I could not bring myself to mention the fact that I had seen Mrs. Larson's murder. He sat in awe-filled silence and listened. I also told him about what I had seen on the trawler with regards to the drug stash, Scar Cheek, and Mr. Larson. I watched his face carefully for any sign that might alert me to his prior knowledge of the drugs, but he seemed genuinely surprised and shook his head vigorously.

"Not Kurt. Kurt would never do something like that. You must have imagined this," he said.

I felt my ire rising and quelled it. "I know what I saw, Mr. Petrov. If I could see Evelyn bury this box then I saw Benny Black and Mr. Larson haul up a crab trap with drug canisters in it."

He stared at me and for a moment I thought he would get up and walk away. He obviously felt conflicted and wanted to believe me, but not the part where his partner might be doing something illegal in their mutual business.

"Okay, say I believe you. What proof can you offer—we have several crab trap sites in the Dolphin Strait.

I smiled for the first time. "I have the coordinates on my phone."

"You had better not be leading me on, Tessa. Let me see the coordinates."

I hauled out my phone and pulled up the information. He squinted at the screen in the overhead light and in a flash came up with the location.

"I know exactly where that is. Do you know what day it was you saw this?"

I thought for a moment. I remember the vision showed a dull day with a lot of wind and dark clouds overhead.

"I saw the vision on Tuesday last week, but we had no bad weather at the time."

Sam interjected. "But we did have a very dull and windy day on Friday last week so that might have been the day they lifted the trap."

It appeared he believed me at last and I breathed a sigh of relief. "It may mean the drugs might have been dropped there that morning," I said.

He thought about it. "The drug canisters must be on the boat somewhere."

"Unless they have got rid of all of them." I told him about how Jinx and I had followed Scar Cheek to the Reardon dealership, whom I suspected of receiving a canister.

A light seemed to go on in Sam's mind. "Okay, now I think I understand things a bit better. Kurt and Gus Reardon have been seeing a lot of each other lately. It's Friday today. I think I will take a trip out to these particular traps and see what I can find."

"So you believe me, then?" I asked.

"The jury is still out on that one, but I guess if I find a trap with drug-filled canisters in it, your story will hold a lot more water. I will also see if there is anything stored away on Kurt's boat."

I stood to go. "You will let me know then—before you do anything else?"

"Why do you ask?"

"I will answer that if, and when, you find the drugs. Bye, Mr. Petrov."

I walked toward the coffee shop's exit and he shouted after me. "Call me Sam."

I raised my hand in acknowledgment and left the premises.

Ж

12

Sam Cooperates

Two days passed before Sam called. It had begun to seem he might have laughed the whole thing off and I worried that a huge mistake had been made in contacting him. I received the call on my cell.

"Tessa? Can we meet again—I have some news for you. The same place at the same time, today, will do if you can make it."

I looked at my watch and felt a tinge of excitement grab me. It was almost two. Things appeared to be falling into place and I raced over to Harvey's to meet with him. We sat in the same back corner booth and sipped on our coffees.

"Did you find anything?" I asked.

He grinned. "You were on the money. I pulled up three traps and in the third one, I found a whole bunch of canisters. It's heroin."

I felt gratified that at last someone besides Jinx believed me and we could figure out a way to secure justice for Mrs. Larson. There remained one thing, though: a move I didn't relish—to tell Sam about Mrs. Larson's murder. This did not sit well with me but I knew it had to be done. I had been right about the drugs, right about the box of letters and Sam's affair with Mrs. Larson. I had to be right about her death and who the murderer was. How else could we move forward?

He looked at me and I detected a certain amount of wonderment in his eyes.

"I never believed in psychics, but now you've proved your point. You said there would be a reason for me to speak to you before I did anything about the drugs. What else have you seen?"

I felt hesitant and my mouth went dry. My lips wanted to stick together and for a brief second my nerve failed me. He detected my reluctance.
"Is it about Evelyn?"

I looked down at my hands and felt a tremble in my chin. I wanted to cry.

"Please tell me, honey. I won't be angry." He reached out a hand and laid it on top of mine in an effort to convey a gesture of comfort. A tear squeezed out and rolled down my cheek. I couldn't look him in the eye.

I nodded.

"Please tell me, Tessa."

I lifted my chin and stared him in the eye. "Evelyn Larson is dead."

He sat in shocked silence and stared at me. His mouth fell open and I could see the sudden pain reflected in his eyes. He shook his head and his voice wavered.

"No." His shoulders slumped and suddenly he looked ten years older. "No, no. It can't be... you're..."

I knew what he meant to say, but couldn't. He wouldn't say I was lying because he knew in his heart it was true.

His hand slipped off mine and he sat in shocked morbidity. I grabbed his hand but he withdrew it and tears began to flow from his eyes. A groan escaped his lips and I could see he agonized at the veracity of my words. His mind, I could see, flittered between the proof of finding the drugs and the fact of the letters and my knowledge of his secret affair. He knew it had to be true, for she had now been missing for at least ten days.

Sam buried his face in shaking hands and tried to subdue his grief. After several minutes he looked up at me. "Tell me what you saw."

"I will tell you as long as you don't react badly and run off to commit a murder yourself."

He nodded.

I told him of my first vision. How Jinx and I had found the old photo of Evelyn and what it had conveyed to me. He waited in shocked silence for me to finish. I told him about Scar Cheek but added that although he committed the murder I didn't think he was behind it. He sat for a long while and then cursed Benny Black's name in the most violent way. When he finished I waited for him to calm down.

I held his glazed stare. "We don't have a body because it was dumped at sea. We have no proof of the murder and I have wondered if we might find it near the crab site. It makes sense to me that they would dispose of the body near the place where they do their fishing."

Still visibly upset, Sam considered my words and with a slow nod of the head, he took control of his feelings.

"You're probably right about Benny. He just follows orders and if Evelyn's body has been dumped at sea then he would have had to have Larson's approval. I am almost certain Kurt didn't know anything about us. They lived two different lives and he didn't really show her any affection. It's one of the reasons her and I became involved. My wife has been going through a menopausal thing for the last two years which made me feel kind of rejected."

"I'm sorry to hear that, but what you did wasn't right," I said.

He dropped his head and for a moment I thought he might burst into tears again.

"I know it was wrong and now I've paid a price for it. We have to find justice for Evelyn."

I felt sorry for him. I could see he felt grieved, but at least I could look forward to someone having the same view as I did about the whole affair.

"What do you think we should do?" I asked.

He thought for a moment and then I sensed a renewed energy in him. "I will go to the police and tell them about the drugs; that I found out by chance and suspected Kurt of being involved. I will also suggest they send divers down to look at the traps and if Evelyn's body is down there they will see it. I assume her corpse would have been wrapped up and weighted for her to have sunk as rapidly as you suggested."

"It may not be that she was wrapped in anything. I had the sense of water bubbles flowing upward before my eyes which might suggest she was not wrapped up, but possibly weighted."

My words caused him to close his eyes.

"I'm sorry. I should choose my words better," I said.

He shook his head. "No, you just said it as you saw it."

"How will you lead the police to believe you stumbled on the drugs? I don't want my dad to know it came from me."

He looked up at the ceiling. "I'll tell them I became suspicious when I found a canister on Kurt's boat while searching for one of the cages I lent him two weeks ago. I then took my boat and checked out his crab sites and found a cage full of canisters. I promise I won't get you into trouble with your dad. Your secret is safe with me."

I must have looked relieved because he gave a glimmer of a smile and took my hand again. "You've done a good thing, Tess. We may be able to solve this whole thing because of what you've seen."

I felt pleased. At long last someone, apart from Jinx, appreciated my gift.

"When will you go and see my dad?" I asked.

"The first thing I will do is search Kurt's boat tonight. I don't want to lie to the police so I will find the canister you said he had in the wheelhouse. Then I will see your dad tomorrow and tell him about the crab site. The police will send out the divers and if Evelyn's body is there, they will find it. I will call you after I have seen your dad."

He talked about how difficult his life had been over the past two years while trying to conduct a secret affair with Evelyn, and now that it had come to an end, he would do everything in his power to make his marriage work again. I felt him to be a good man at heart and had I been older I wouldn't have minded exploiting the weakness in his marriage. I knew from the Internet search on his name that he had to be in his early forties. We said goodbye and I drove home feeling quite good about myself. In a way, I had succeeded in passing on the baton, and at last, justice would come for Evelyn Larson.

*

I didn't recall much about the following day. I lived in a twilight world of fantasy and the night after our meeting, dreamed that Sam Petrov had come to my bed to kiss me. My dad didn't mention there had been a change in the status of the case because I think he wanted me to stay out of police business. I received a call from Sam on the second day, following our meeting at Harvey's. The call came during one of Miss Bennett's lessons and I had to make an excuse to go to the bathroom in order to receive it. Sam's voice sounded steady.

"I found the canister in Kurt's boat—the one you saw in your vision, but I left it in its place. I then went to see your dad and told him about my suspicions. He questioned the life out of me to make sure I wasn't turning my partner in so I could pin Evelyn's disappearance on someone. He thought I might be involved in the drug smuggling business myself, but in the end, I think he believed me."

I commiserated with Sam. "I know exactly what you must have gone through. I love my dad, but he does tend to be suspicious of everyone—it's just the cop in him."

He gave a brief chuckle. "I guess being a cop's daughter is not easy. He did promise to send two cops to check Kurt's trawler and divers to the crab site. He didn't want to use the divers at first, but I told him he might find more than just drugs and it would be wise to do so."

"Perhaps he connected the dots and realized that Mr. Larson might be involved in his wife's disappearance—that she may have been murdered and disposed of," I said.

"Your dad has told me not to leave town. By now, they will have checked Kurt's boat and found the canister so the fishing side of the business will come to a stop until I'm cleared of wrongdoing," he said.

"And he doesn't suspect my involvement?" I asked.

"Your name never came up. I promise you."

I felt a relief. "What about your cell phone call log? Won't they be able to track your calls? They'll know you have called me."

"I am using an unregistered phone. It's the one I always used to contact Evelyn. Her phone, also unregistered, was in the small box you found."

"Will Mr. Larson know it was you who turned him in?"

"Not unless the police tell him. They have no reason to do so because they will find the drugs on his boat and he will have difficulty in explaining that away. He'll be arrested and probably released on bail unless they find Evelyn's body at the crab site."

"So, we wait to see what the divers come up with?" I asked.

"We wait. I will still be a person of suspicion but because that particular crab site is Kurt's normal responsibility—the finger of suspicion will be pointing at him."

"I will ask him tonight if there has been any change in the status of the case. Sometimes he shares snippets of information with me. I'll let you know."

The rest of the day passed in a foggy daze for me. Would the divers find the body? Only time would tell. That evening I prepared my dad's favorite food, handed him his newspaper, gave a long hug and kiss on the cheek, poured his pre-meal glass of whiskey and as he sat to relax for a few moments, popped the question.

"Has there been any advancement in the Lar-son Case?"

Ж

13

The Body Bag

My dad smiled and lowered the newspaper to eye me with a "now I know why you were so nice to me" look.

"You know I can't share details of an ongoing investigation, don't you?"

"I know, dad, but you know how much I want justice for Mrs. Larson."

"We all want justice, honey. I still can't talk about the case, but I will say this: we have made significant progress and I wouldn't be surprised if we solve it soon."

"That's so good to know," I said. My cell rang and I saw Jinx's name come up.

"I'll take this call from Jinx and then dinner will be served."

He buried himself in the newspaper again so I hurried off to my room. Twaddle with his favorite toy clenched between his teeth and feeling a little neglected barged passed me to jump onto the bed in demand of a game. The toy, a short length of smelly, old rope was used for a tug-of-war with whoever would fall for his trick. I sat down on the bed and grabbed one end of the rope to his delight, and tried to continue a conversation with Jinx.

"So, what've you like, been up to? Haven't seen you for like, a couple of days, dude."

I felt a little bad about having kept him out of the loop, as we always shared what was going on in our lives. I told him what had transpired since my trip to the botanical gardens and he expressed delight at the progress.

"I've been doing like, a little snooping of my own."

"What have you discovered?" I asked.

"Can we like, talk tomorrow. POS."

He indicated in millennial speak that his parents were listening.

"Okay, I'll pick you up tomorrow after school and we can go to the quarry."

No sooner had I finished the conversation than my messaging "binged". It was Bree.

Have you heard?

I typed the answer. *No, whaddap?*

Down at main wharf to pick up my dad...police boat came in...Divers on board...They took off a body bag.

A tingle of excitement. I answered. *Body bag?*

Dad spoke to the police...they think the missing woman from last week...so exciting.

Bree's father, a cabinetmaker, worked as a contractor on luxury yachts. She would have gone to pick him up at the end of a day's work and the yachts were all parked adjacent to the police mooring. The pieces of the puzzle now fell into place and soon the noose would tighten around Kurt Larson's and Benny Black's, necks. I had no doubt in my mind Mr. Larson was the ultimate guilty party.

Dad and I made small talk as we ate dinner and after watching telly for two hours, I decided to turn in. Twaddle made a nuisance of himself as usual and grabbed the ride from off my prosthetic foot as I tried to remove it. After a wild chase around the bed and over the top of it, I managed to grab hold of him and remove said footwear from his jaws. Sheba hissed and spat at him every time we passed her by in the pursuit. With lights out, things calmed down and the animals assumed their sleeping positions. It took some time for my mind to come to rest.

*

I zipped out of the house the moment Miss Bennett left and drove over to Jinx's place. He had been waiting and we left for the quarry. Twaddle, happy to be included, jammed in between the two seats and made a general nuisance of himself with cough-like barks and sporadic licks.

We walked to the ledge and sat on the rock surface, our attention taken by a flock of geese taking off from the tranquil waters. I knew Jinx would be waiting patiently for me to ask what he had been up to.

"You said you've been doing some snooping around—whaddap?"

He beamed. "I decided to check on the dealership....." He paused for effect.

"Go on, Bond," I said. It always helped to butter him up a little.

"I saw Scar Cheek arrive and like, wait for Mr. Reardon."

"Where were you?"

"Doing just what Bond would have done, dude."

I waited for an explanation.

"I was hiding in a group of like, floor fixtures... plastic palm trees in containers and no one knew I was like, there."

"What did they talk about?"

"Mr. Reardon told Scar Cheek to like, chill. Scar Cheek seemed worried."

"Worried about what?" I asked.

"Worried that they would like, find out he had murdered Mrs. Larson."

"You're saying that Gus Reardon is also involved in her murder?"

"It seemed like it might be so."

I considered the implications of Reardon's involvement. "Did they mention anything else?"

"Mrs. Larson like, apparently found out about the drugs."

Things began to fall into place. If Mrs. Larson found out about the drug smuggling business, she might have been ready to blow the whistle, so they killed her. It made sense. But was it Reardon or Kurt Larson who made that decision?

"Bree texted me last night. She had gone to pick her dad up from work, down at the main wharf, and they saw the harbor police take a body bag off their boat. It has to be Mrs. Larson's body. When I asked my dad earlier, he wouldn't share anything with me except that they had made significant progress."

"Has Mr. Larson been arrested yet?"

"I think he may have been by now. Sam said the police wanted to see if the body was at the crab site first."

"How do we like, tie Mr. Reardon and Scar Cheek to the murder?"

"It certainly seems that both Mr. Reardon and Mr. Larson are involved up to their eyeteeth. If I could get something personal of Mr. Reardon's, he may give away something important, which could be used to expose him."

"You can leave it to Bond."

"What are you thinking, 'James?'" I asked.

Jinx blushed and glanced at the ground, then looked up at my face with an inquiring frown. "Bond will easily get anything you like, need, dude."

"Don't place yourself at risk, 'James.' I don't want you to get hurt."

"Bond always knows what he's like, doing. Don't worry about a thing."

Jinx was so vain. I really didn't want him to stick his neck out for this but at the same time, if I could touch any object which belonged to Mr. Reardon—

"Do you need a ride to the dealership?"

"Let's go," he said.

We drove to Reardon's Dealership and I parked down the street. Twaddle jumped into the passenger seat to keep me company while we waited for James Bond to do his thing. I needn't have worried about Jinx. He would have made an excellent operative for any information gathering business. Thirty minutes later, he came skipping along whistling the James Bond signature soundtrack.

Twaddle vacated the seat and jumped into the back with a joyful cough, his tail spinning like a propeller. I didn't see anything in Jinx's hands.

"Did you manage to find something?"

"Yep." He grinned and pulled out an object from his pocket. "Bond does it again."

I laughed and then glanced at what he held in his hand—a small, black notebook.

"That looks very interesting," I said. "Well done, 'James.'"

He tilted his head back and made that awful clucking which sent Twaddle into a spasm of cough-like barks. On arrival at Jinx's home, he got out of the jeep and placed the notebook into the jeep's glove compartment.

"Let me know what like, happens."

"You'll be the first person I call."

"Bye Felicia," he said.

I drove away with a feeling of excitement and couldn't help a shout of glee. Twaddle's ears pricked up and he did that grin thing.

*

After dinner, Dad settled down in front of the telly and I decided it to be a good time to see what Mr. Reardon had been up to. After some brief texting with Bree and Jan about latest movie star escapades, I picked up the notebook, lay down on my bed and paged through it. There were numerous numbers with dollar signs written down on the pages, plus names of what could have been sales staff. Then I came across one page with a date on it and next to it a name—Sam Petrov. The date was prior to the day of which Mrs. Larson went missing. I understood there to have been a meeting between Gus Reardon and Sam Petrov on the date in the notebook. What did Reardon have to do with Petrov? A gnawing feeling started in my gut and a sudden disappointment engulfed me.

It was normal when looking for psychic transportation that I relax my body completely and concentrate my thoughts on the target of my research, but having just seen Sam's name connected with Reardon upset me. After several moments of second-guessing my meetings with Sam, I managed to calm down enough to begin my psychic journey. Twaddle lay at my feet, his doleful eyes locked onto my vacant stare. Sheba came up close and I could hear her purr as she sought to brush against the side of my face, but my mind had already interfaced with another realm.

A swirling mist engulfed me and as it dissipated, I found myself in an office seated across a desk, looking intently at the face of the man seated opposite me. The face I could see shook me to the core. It was Sam Petrov. Perspiration trickled down his forehead, where a vein stuck out like a rope. I saw him open his mouth to speak and the words expressed came with slow deliberation. I couldn't understand at first, but each word sank into my consciousness as I watched his lips move in slow motion.

"You...can't...allow...this...to...happen...Gus."

Then the mist swirled in again and engulfed the scene. A moment later I came to, still lying on my bed with my head on the pillow and Sheba brushing up against my cheek. Her fur tickled my nose as feeling surged back into my body and I pushed her away from me. Twaddle lifted his head in alarm and made a lunge at Sheba, but she sprang into the air to land on the floor, all a-bristle. Twaddle swooped down on her and they both ended up under the bed in a face-off of snarling and hissing.

I regained control of my senses and admonished both of them. Twaddle crept out from under the bed, tail between legs and Sheba shot out the other side, up onto my dresser, where she stood defiantly with the wagging tail. I relaxed and contemplated the vision. It didn't tell me much—only that Sam and Mr. Reardon had met together days before Evelyn disappeared. I couldn't gather anything concrete from the words expressed. What was Sam trying to convey to Reardon? What could Reardon not allow to happen?

One thing it did tell me, however: Sam was more involved in this whole thing than just the affair with Evelyn. My heart felt sore. I had believed in his innocence and in our limited meetings had grown to like him, even felt a tinge of romantic attachment despite the difference in our ages. I might have lost my ally and as much as it hurt, I now needed to treat Sam with suspicion again.

I reached for my phone and sent a text to Jinx.

I was wrong about Sam. He is involved. I can't even.

A question came back a few seconds later. *Do we need to cancel him?*

I thought about it for a second. *Not entirely. We need to be wary of him. It's awks.*

Jinx answered. *Perf. Whatever you say. We're fam.*

I felt tired and decided to end off. *Bye, Felicia. Talk to ya tomorrow.*

Perf.

I was going out of my mind.

Ж

14

A Visit to the Boatyard

I awoke the next morning not knowing why I felt such a lump in my throat. Then I remembered the previous evening's vision. Sheba lay stretched out next to me and as I moved, she placed a paw on my cheek, as if to apologize for her antics the previous evening. Twaddle's tail thumped on the bed and his eyes also seemed to search for my forgiveness. I patted the bed for permission for him to crawl up closer and roughed his ears while I rubbed my cheek against Sheba's. My animals meant the world to me and although I often rebuked them, I didn't know what would happen to me if they were no longer a part of my life.

My mind returned to the Larson case and I tried to think of what the next course of action should be but drew a blank. With exasperation, I threw back the bed covers, got up, grabbed my prosthesis and hopped out toward the bathroom for a shower. Later at breakfast, dad seemed preoccupied and I could see the mental gears churning.

"What's on your mind, dad?"

Shocked out of his reverie, he glanced up from his boiled egg. "Oh, nothing much. I have a busy day ahead of me. I have some bad news and perhaps I should tell you now before the newspapers proclaim it to the world."

"Mrs. Larson's body's been found, hasn't it?"

"How did you guess?"

"Bree texted me last night to say that she and her dad saw a body bag being taken from the police boat. It could only have been Mrs. Larson."

I could thank Bree for supplying me with the "foreknowledge," to the truth I'd already known for over a week.

"It was her. Kurt Larson positively identified her body."

"Do you think he had something to do with her murder?" I asked.

"He remains a suspect along with a half-dozen others, but I can't discuss it."

I feigned disappointment in him not being able to share the details but the fact was I knew far more about the whole thing than the police did. "I understand," I said.

"Have to get going. I don't even have my weekends off while this case remains unsolved." He got up from the table, gave me the usual peck on the head then grabbed his phone and made for the door. "See you tonight."

Saturdays were usually the days I caught up on my social media and posted things on Facebook. Bree and Jan both sent texts to meet at the mall for lunch, but I declined, citing the housework. My mind needed the time to be preoccupied with the details of the case. I sent a text to Jinx and told him to be ready for a strategy meeting in the afternoon at the old quarry, then started on the laundry.

*

I picked up Jinx and we drove out to the old quarry with Twaddle jammed between us as he always was when in the Jeep. I wanted to run an idea past Jinx and as soon as we were seated on the ledge, I launched into my proposal.

"We need to get some clarity on Sam Petrov and find a way to expose the real murderer. I remember something Sam told me about his affair with Evelyn—they used unregistered phones. I also remember seeing her cell phone in the box with the letters. If we could find either of the phones, we may be able to find out more about his involvement in Evelyn's death."

Jinx gave the matter some thought and then came up with a problem. "The phone's will...um, more than likely be...um, password protected."

I hadn't thought of that. Trust Jinx to bring up the obvious. "We could see that my dad gets them," I said.

"Or...um, if you, like, leave it to...um, Bond—."

"What are you suggesting?"

"I...um, have a good buddy, who...um, like, knows how to do passwords and...um, stuff."

"You always manage to surprise me, 'James.'"

"Glad you're...um, like, getting to know my... um, capabilities. Where...um, do you think these... um, phones will, like, be?"

"He wouldn't keep them at his home but I think he might use his trawler as a safe place to hide things."

"That's...um, the bigger of the two...um, boats?"

"We need to get onto the boat and search. I'm sure we'll find the box, at the very least."

Jinx became quiet and I thought him to be thinking of a reason for us not to do it, but he was thinking ahead of me. "One of us should...um, go onto the vessel, while the...um, other keeps, like, watch."

"You're right, 'James.' I will go on the boat since I know what the box and the phone look like. You can keep watch."

"Are you sure you...um, don't want Bond doing the...um, snooping?"

"You've done more than your fair share. This is on me," I said.

"When do you want to...um, like, do this?"

"With Mr. Larson's arrest and Sam still under suspicion, the trawlers are not operating at the moment. Both will be at the boatyard wharf and it being the weekend the other staff will also be away.

Jinx's mind still kept ticking over on the safety issue of our mission. "If anything...um should happen to you...um, what would you...um, want me to do?"

"Call my dad. It's the only thing."

"Perf. Let's...um, hope none of the...um, boat-yard wankstas are, like, around."

"The office is closed on Saturday afternoons, so there shouldn't be anyone—I'll be cool."

We left the quarry after a short game with Twaddle. I wanted to drop him off at home, just on the off-chance something did happen to me. I parked the Jeep, took him into my bedroom and closed the door. If I didn't make it home, my dad would find Twaddle in the bedroom and suspect something to be wrong. It was not something I could envisage but to have a backup plan, no matter how shaky, struck me as being a good thing.

I trooped back out to the Jeep to Twaddle's muffled cough-barking and felt a twinge of guilt at leaving him behind—should have taken him with me, but at the time I didn't have an inkling of what lay ahead.

*

We sat in the Jeep, parked outside the deserted boatyard, and built up courage for the impending mission. I felt nervous and made an effort to put on a brave front. Maybe I should have let Jinx do the snooping but he had done more than his fair share. If I found the box and the phones, he would be the one to take it from there in finding the passwords. If his friend could not do it, I would have no other choice but to send the box and its contents to the police. This might be the better course of action to follow, but I couldn't resist wanting to know all the details about Sam. It had become personal.

The afternoons had turned cooler and fall appeared to be well on its way. I turned up the collar of my windbreaker and pulled the cap lower over my eyes. Jinx sat there with an impassive look on his face, unfazed by the enormity of the task that lay ahead of us.

"I'm going now. Where will you keep watch?" I asked.

"I'll...um, hide over there between those...um, two, like repair jobs." He pointed to a group of small wooden skiffs on chocks, a short distance from the big trawler. "If anyone...um, comes along, I'll, like, give my...um, bird whistle."

With our watch details sorted, I walked into the boatyard with Jinx trailing me and made straight for the large trawler. The smaller boat had yellow police tape all over it because of the drug investigation. The overhead cloud cover cast a gloomy scene over the yard and I became aware of shadows. The place seemed deathly quiet and I began to imagine all sorts of things. Jinx's presence, however, lifted my bravado and I took heart at the fact that no one else should be around at that time on a Saturday.

He settled himself between the two repair jobs and his voice floated across the wharf. "Bye, Felicia, yolo."

To remind me I only lived once was perhaps not Jinx's finest moment, but he never gave much thought to such things. The boards of the wharf creaked as I walked on them and climbed over the boat's gunnel onto the deck. From the boatyard article I had gathered, this trawler was new and boasted a lot of modern equipment, a fact that really meant nothing to me at the time. As I walked on the deck, however, I became conscious of how firm and new the floor-plates were with brightly painted white and yellow lines, to signify walking or storage areas. I made for the housing near the stern where the top of a flight of stairs became visible, which I assumed, led to the cabins and stor-age below deck.

My rides made no sound as I took each step down into the depths of the vessel and the dark-ness that awaited me. It took several minutes for my eyes to adjust to the gloom and at the bottom of the stairs, I found myself looking down a corri-dor with several metal doors leading off on each side. At the end I could see another flight of steps leading upward, I assumed to the wheelhouse. I made my way along the corridor looking in at each small room. One a little larger than the rest con-tained several sleeping berths for staff while at sea. Another appeared to be a personal cabin, like a captain's stateroom and a surge of excitement took hold of me as I entered.

On the wall, I saw a picture of Sam Petrov and his wife and I knew I was in the right place. A wooden cabinet with drawers caught my attention so a quick search of the contents ensued, but noth-ing came up. Next, I spotted a closet that seemed to contain jackets, oilskins, and gumboots for bad weather. There were a few drawers but these re-vealed nothing of any importance. I cursed myself for not bringing a flashlight; it would have made the search easier. I pressed on, however, and when nothing else appeared to be worthy of investiga-tion, I looked up and saw a gap between the top of the closet and the ceiling. A quick feel with my hand revealed a small box. My excitement reached a new height and I pulled the box out of its hiding place—it was the box containing the love notes from Sam. Inside were two cell phones with the letters. I couldn't believe my luck.

A few minutes later I made my way back along the corridor to the steps and skipped up to the top with the box held firmly in my two hands.

At the top of the stairs, I stepped onto the deck and with sudden force, a pair of strong hands grasped me from behind. I got such a fright that I wet my pants. The box clattered to the ground and I felt my body being turned around to face the perpetrator—Scar Cheek. There was no way to describe what went through my mind. In that moment, I believed I was going to die.

Ж

15

Fearfully Incarcerated

Fear accompanied by the urge to vomit up my lunch had me totally owned as he dragged my body down into the bowels of the ship. No scream or sound came from my lips, only dry gasps for air as I bumped and thumped down the stairs behind him. He took no care for my wellbeing. A moment later he hurled me into a small room and I heard the clang of an iron gate. The metal floor felt hard and cold against the skin of my cheek. By the sound of his voice, I knew it was Scar Cheek.

He laughed and said he would be back later for some "fun". I shuddered to think what that meant. A quick look around in the gloom revealed a cell-like room with a wooden bench.

His footsteps reverberated down the corridor and my nerves gave way to wails and sobs. I must have looked like an emo or worse—never been so afraid in all my life. Then came the clang of the metal door at the bottom of the stairs. It sounded so final. I picked myself up off the floor, grabbed the bars and shook the gate with all my strength—solid as the rock of Gibraltar. I stared at the wrought iron verticals—there appeared to be only one option for an escape, but I had never done metal this thick before.

I backed off a little, wiped the tears from my eyes and concentrated on a single bar in the gate. The rise of energy within me coalesced into a single flow of force as all my mental power came to bear. After several minutes I collapsed on the floor. It hadn't worked.

I wondered about Jinx. Did he realize what had just happened and how would he react? It seemed to me, as I thought about it, Scar Cheek must have been on the boat before I came aboard. He would have heard me searching Sam's cabin and then waited for me at the top of the stairs. A pang of fear rampaged through me again as I realized Jinx would not have been able to see the stairs from his hideaway. He probably still sat out there waiting for me to come out. Panic seized me. What if Scar Cheek saw us enter the boatyard. He might have seen where Jinx had hidden. My fears were realized when I heard cursing and swearing accompany the clang of the door at the bottom of the stairs, as someone opened and dragged what sounded like a heavy sack along the floor of the corridor. It had to be Scar Cheek returning and he pulled something along with him. The gate to my cell opened and a body came tumbling in. The gate then clanged shut and I heard the key grate in the lock.

Jinx jumped to his feet and cursed in a way I've never heard before. There were words I didn't even know existed coming from his mouth. Scar Cheek reached through the bars and grabbed him by the front of his shirt.

"I'll be back when I've spoken to the boss," he said.

Jinx fell back onto his haunches and cursed a bit more until he realized he wasn't alone.

"Tess...geez, you like, scared the crap out of me."

"How did he find you?" I asked. My voice shook like a true emo.

Jinx looked a bit crestfallen. "I never like, saw him. He crept up behind me. I didn't see where the dickhead like, came from and the next thing I like, knew, he was all over me. How about you?"

I told him how Scar Cheek caught me at the top of the stairs. I frowned. "You didn't see him get off the boat? He must have been watching you."

"I was like, looking at the yard's entrance all the time—never saw him coming."

"He said he would be back. We have to figure a way out of here."

Jinx grabbed the bars again. "You have that way of bending things, Tess. Can't you like, give it a go?"

I felt my shoulders slump. "I've tried. I think the bars are too thick for me."

"Can't you like, try again? Remember when you were like, trying that thick rebar in your dad's garage?"

I remembered the incident. I was showing off my gift to Jinx and the piece of rebar I used was thick. I had tried three consecutive times until it began to move.

"I was younger then. Perhaps my powers are dwindling."

"Come on dude. You can do it. I like, know you can."

His insistence spurred me on to give it another try. I could see no other way out and if Scar Cheek returned with whoever gave the orders, we would be toast.

"Stand in the corner," I ordered. With one vertical bar in mind I came up close and pressed my cheek against the adjacent bars so that if it did move, it would bend toward its neighbor. I began to think of all the things that made me really angry. I thought of my dad when he belittled my talk of psychic powers. I thought about the circumstances that ripped my mom from my life and then I thought of Scar Cheek with his hands around Mrs. Larson's throat. I could feel the anger rise within me and in its wake, something much more formidable—an overwhelming source of universal, cosmic energy.

My eyes began to burn as I concentrated my stare onto the vertical bar before me. The room seemed to disappear and my surroundings vanished. Perspiration beaded on my forehead and my stump began to pain in a way I had not experienced before. My joints started to ache and my stomach hurt as the power within me increased to a high level of intensity. In my mind's eye, I held the vertical bar in clear focus and imagined the bar bending. Thirty seconds passed and my body, drenched in perspiration, began to sag. I felt hands grab me from behind—it was Jinx.

"Don't give up dude. It's beginning to like, bend."

I heard his voice far off in space somewhere, but it encouraged me to concentrate. The strange power within me built up to the point where I thought I may pass out. Then Jinx shouted, again.

"It's bending—don't stop."

I kept my focus for what seemed an eternity and then it became too much and I flopped backward into Jinx's arms. He allowed me to slide down onto the cell's floor and it took a while before I could concentrate again. The sound of his voice coaxing me to wake up grew louder until I became fully conscious of my surroundings again. I sat up.

"You slew it, Tess. Like, look at that bar." He pointed toward the gate and I noticed the difference in the verticals. One of them made a neat semi-circle, the middle section of which touched against its neighbor.

I felt tired, as though I had run a marathon, and my stump hurt.

A pang of disappointment hit me as I looked at the size of the gap. "It's not big enough for us to get through."

Jinx would not be put off. "If you...um, move this bar in the...um opposite direction it will make a space big enough for me to like, squeeze through, I'm sure."

I couldn't imagine going through all that again, but in the end, I knew there would be no other choice. When Scar Cheek returned, it would all be over. Being back on my feet again brought a round of dizziness and it took several moments for me to regain my composure for a second onslaught on the next vertical. It did not take as long this time, at least, not that I thought. A while later I lay on the ground again in a semi-coma with Jinx shouting words into my ear. He sounded very far away at first and the sound of his voice became louder. After another round of dizziness, I looked up at the verticals to see the extent of my handiwork. A neat circle pattern in the targeted bars and Jinx, the smaller of the two of us, already had his head through. I looked in amazement as he struggled and squirmed until his shoulders passed, then his hips and finally, he fell out of the cell onto the other side of the gate.

I couldn't have been happier. I knew I would never get through the gap, though.

"Great work, Jinx. I won't make it, so our lives are in your hands."

"I'll get your dad," he said.

"Do you know how to drive?" I fished the Jeep's keys out of my jean's pocket.

"I've like, driven my dad's truck a few times on an open road. I'll manage."

"Just put it in 'drive', and remember to take the handbrake off. It's an automatic and as long as you know where the brakes are, you'll be okay."

"Bond. knows."

"Get going, then, James," I shouted.

He ran off down the corridor toward the closed metal door at the bottom of the stairs and opened it. With a quick peek, he slipped through and disappeared.

I sagged down onto my haunches with my back against the cell's wall and contemplated the possibilities. Then, it became too much for me and I fell forward onto my stomach and cried my heart out.

*

I had no idea how long it was before I heard a sound at the end of the corridor. I woke from a deep sleep, in shock of my surroundings before I remembered. It all came back to me with a rush of fear. My only hope lay in a fifteen-year-old boy who thought he was James Bond. Jinx would have been considered a wanksta if he had not been my best buddy. Now he represented my only hope of survival.

I heard voices. One, I recognized as Scar Cheeks, but the other sounded a little muffled. Scar Cheek sounded angry and surprised at the same time. "I left this door closed."

The other voice, still a little indistinct, sounded familiar. "I hope they haven't escaped."

"They couldn't get through the gate. I locked it," answered Scar Cheek.

A light went on in the center of the corridor and at last, I could see everything around me clearly.

I got off the floor and sat on the wooden bench against one of the adjacent walls, out of the view of the two villains. They approached and then stopped. Scar Cheek let out a curse when he saw the two verticals bent out of their normal shape.

"That's impossible. They're just kids," he shouted.

They came up to the gate and peered into the cell. I held their gaze, but my eyes fell on the second person. I took a deep breath—Sam Petrov. I began to shake.

"We meet again, Tessa."

I stared at him in horror and words failed me.

"Where's your nerdy friend?" Sam asked.

"You'd better release me, this minute, Sam. Jinx has gone to get my dad."

The two men looked at each other, then Petrov spoke. "No matter. It's your young friend's word against ours. We'll swear we never laid eyes on you —besides who'll believe a rough kid from the wrong side of the tracks? What I don't understand is how he bent those bars."

"It's none of your business, now let me go."

He laughed. "Not this time, honey. You know far too much about our business."

"You killed Mrs. Larson because she found out about your drug business, and now you're going to kill me." My voice carried a quiver and exposed my fear.

"Actually, I didn't kill Evelyn—Benny here did that on Gus Reardon's orders. I was opposed to it, but we couldn't allow the business to be exposed."

"You loved her. You should have protected her," I sputtered.

His eyes hardened. "Yes, I did love her but Kurt was about to find out and that would have been the end of the business for me. We did what had to be done. He is going to take the fall for the drug operation and killing his own wife. He just doesn't know it yet."

"You're a monster, Petrov," I shouted.

"Save the moral speech, honey. It's unfortunate, but you have to pay the price for your meddling. Benny, cast us off—we're going on a short fishing trip."

Scar Cheek grinned and raked my body with his filthy eyes. "Like I said before, darlin...I'll be back to have some fun."

Ж

16

A Close Call

I lost the concept of time. All I could think about was the return of Scar Cheek. I knew his intentions. After a while, I started thinking about Twaddle, Sheba, and also my dad. Jinx would have succeeded in telling him the story by now, but with the trawler out at sea he would have to mount a police search. It seemed I was about to share Mrs. Larson's fate, but much worse when Benny Black returned to have his way with me. I removed my prosthesis, determined to use it as a weapon. I would go down fighting.

The door, which serviced the stairs to the wheelhouse, opened and Petrov stepped into the corridor. He came to stand at the gate. In his hand, he held the wooden box that contained all the details of his affair with Evelyn Larson. He took out one of the cell phones. "I assume you were after this?"

I glared at him but said nothing.

"No one will ever find these again after I drop them overboard—just thought you should know."

I turned my head away and couldn't stop the tears from falling. After a few seconds, I found my voice. "So, you and Mr. Reardon from the motor dealership decided to have Evelyn killed when she found out about the drugs. Was Mr. Larson in on the plan to kill her?"

"No. She did have it out with him, though, and he tried to convince her not to go to the authorities but she wouldn't listen. He was at a loss, so Reardon and I stepped in to do what had to be done. He didn't know about our decision."

I wiped my eyes with the back of a hand. "But you loved her."

"I did, but I was not prepared to throw my whole life overboard—she was going to the authorities."

"You took me in for a while there in the coffee shop, but I saw you and Reardon arguing about something."

"You paid us a psychic visit? How nice of you, honey. I did try to find another way, but he was insistent."

"And you're prepared to kill me, as well?"

"I have no choice."

"You won't get away with it. My dad will be out looking for me and he will find the trawler—you will pay." I suddenly felt calm.

"He may find me, but he won't find you. Not where we are going to dump you."

His eyes hardened and he turned back to the stairs. "As I said: our word against that of a young ruffian's will stand better in court—if it comes down to that." He turned the light off and I heard his steps clang like death-knells as he clumped up the stairs.

Darkness gripped me with icy fingers and I felt a general numbness throughout my body. My thoughts returned to the animals and dad, but there were no consolations. By the time my dad caught up with the trawler, I would be dead. The sound I dreaded the most came from the opposite end of the corridor as the door clanged open and the light blinded my eyes. Scar Cheek sidled up to the gate and stared down at me. I grasped the prosthesis tighter and waited for him. After raking my body again with those leering eyes, he smiled and unlocked the gate. He stood there after opening it, staring at me and then slowly began to undo the buckle of his belt.

I raised the prosthetic leg to shoulder height and waited. He seemed oblivious of the leg and started to advance into the cell. As he came within striking distance, I swung the leg at him with all the strength I could muster. He caught it with his one hand and held it while I squirmed and tried to tear it away. His wicked grin revealed tobacco-stained teeth and I could see spittle forming at the corners of his mouth. His strength overcame my efforts to free the leg and he tore it out of my hands. He grabbed my arm and his fingers bit into my flesh like steel claws. I struggled with all my strength to get free, but it was all to no avail. His breath wafted down into my space and I wanted to throw up. Then Sam Petrov called out from the wheelhouse.

"We have a problem, Benny. Come quickly."

He hesitated for a moment and then smiled. His hand slipped onto my breasts and I thought he was going to rip my windbreaker off. Then he removed his hand and let me go with a push, which caused me to fall back against the cell wall.

"Coming," he yelled.

He left the cell and locked the gate. Relief flooded through me like a river and I took a huge breath into my lungs. As he clumped up the stairs toward the wheelhouse, I heard a familiar drone— it sounded like a helicopter. A moment later, Scar Cheek raced back down the stairs to appear at the gate again. "You're coming with me," he shouted.

He dragged me along the corridor to the back stairs and out onto the deck. In the failing light, I could see the helicopter hovering about twenty feet off the surface, side on with the door open and two police officers with weapons pointed at us. I was gratified to see the sight but I realized why Benny Black had brought me out to the deck. He pulled me to the far-side gunwale and held me in a tight grip.

A third person appeared at the open door of the chopper—I recognized my dad, in his black S.W.A.T type clothing. He had a loudhailer in his hand.

"Release your hostage, immediately," he shouted.

Scar Cheek leaned over the gunnel, pulling me with him and keeping his body behind mine. We leaned dangerously off-balance and I feared the two of us might topple into the sea at any moment.

My dad shouted his message through the loudhailer again. "Release the hostage or you will be killed."

Scar Cheek grimaced and held onto me tightly. I could feel the spray from the sea hit my face as I looked down into its depths below. A bright light switched on, bathing us in its glow as I heard a shot ring out. The next thing I knew, I felt the coldness of the water as I hit it headfirst. Scar Cheek released his hold on me and I floated up to the surface with much spluttering and coughing. The water felt icy against my skin and I tried to stay afloat, but my clothes filled with water and started to drag me down. I realized for the first time I was going to drown. Air bubbles streamed upwards from my mouth as I began to sink into the dark, murky depths. For a moment I recognized the vision from my first encounter with Evelyn as she sank under the surface. *So this is what it's like to drown,* I thought.

All of a sudden a strong hand gripped me and I turned to see my mom's face staring at me in wonder. She smiled as if welcoming me to her world and then my head broke the surface. I heard my dad's voice.

"I've got you, cupcake. You'll be safe now."

I must have passed out because I didn't remember anything further about the rescue. I regained consciousness in the hospital almost an hour and a half later.

A bright, overhead light shone in my eyes and a man wearing spectacles and a white coat, looked down at me. "Welcome back to the land of the living, Tessa."

Relief flooded my being. "Am I alive?" I asked.

The doctor grinned and felt my pulse. "You're going to live for a long, long time. You will be fine."

My dad peered down at me from the opposite side. "I'm so glad to see you, sweetheart."

"Not nearly as glad as I was to see you in the chopper," I said."

"How're you feeling?" he asked.

"Like I've been dead, but now I'm alive."

He frowned. "We have some talking to do."

"I know, dad—just not right now. I'm too tired."

I wasn't really too tired. I didn't want to get into the whole thing until I had found time to think things over. I needed to know what Jinx had told my dad to start with. I looked toward the wall and there he sat with a huge grin on his face.

"Hey, 'James,'" I said.

He beamed and went red. "Bond...um, like, did it again," was all he could muster.

I nodded and chuckled. My dad and the doctor looked puzzled.

"Just a little joke we have between us," I said.

17

Summing things Up

I spent the night under observation and my dad came to get me the next day. We drove out to a place called "land's end" where he parked at the view site.

"I don't know what I would have done if I'd lost you, honey." I could see tears forming in his eyes and the last thing I wanted was for him to go emo on me.

"It came close," I said.

"I have many questions about why you were in the hands of those thugs."

"What did Jinx tell you?" I asked.

"He said I should ask you. I got nothing out of him. What is with that kid? He can hardly speak the English language."

I went quiet for a moment. "What he doesn't know about communicating is made up with his good heart."

"We've apprehended Sam Petrov, who gave us another name—Gus Reardon. But then I guess you already knew about that. It seems that Reardon ordered Benny Black to take Mrs. Larson out of the picture, but, somehow, I assume you knew that as well."

Not sure if his words were sarcasm I reacted predictably. "What are you saying, dad?"

"Oh, nothing. You just seem to know a hell of a lot more than you're letting on."

"Really?" I gave him my most innocent look.

"And...there's another thing that puzzles me. Down in the trawler there was a small room with an iron gate and I assume they kept you there. Two of the gate's bars were bent in a way that might have allowed a kid the size of Jinx to squeeze through."

"You don't say," I retorted.

"Don't get cute with me, young lady."

"I'm not getting cute, dad. I just don't know anything about it."

He stared at me and then smiled. "Okay, okay. Enough questions. We should get home. Your animals are running amuck and I would hate for them to destroy the house.

"I have one question," I stated.

He looked pensively at me. "What, honey?"

"The man with the scar on his cheek, Benny Black—what happened to him?"

Dad went quiet and then his eyes lit up. "You won't have to ever worry about him again, sweetheart. We pulled his body out of the sea moments after we rescued you."

"Thanks," I said.

"For what?"

"For rescuing me. For being there when I needed you most, and for laying off all the questions."

He leaned over and hugged me. "I do have one more question for you, though."

"What?" I asked.

"How the hell did James Bond get involved in all this?"

We both laughed. Dad turned the key in the ignition and we pulled out of the parking area. I looked forward to seeing Twaddle and Sheba again.

THE END

More Books by Adeline Setterfield

Tessa: Ghosts of the Klondike.

.

www.ingramcontent.com/pod-product-compliance
Lightning Source LLC
Chambersburg PA
CBHW021059130626
46552CB00005B/2184